SUDDEN STRATEGY

Harrumph heaved a sigh, a sound not unlike the death rattle of a rhino. "Ssuch pity; yoursself, and Ssean and all his Terriess—and I as well—musst die, all for the vainglory of one madman. If I could get my handss on hiss sscrawny neck..."

He clacked his chelae together with a sharp report.

"That might be fun," Retief said. "But how would it help our present situation?"

"Well, it..." Harrumph began, then broke off, looked thoughtfully at Retief, his saucer eyes gleaming in the dark. "As a matter of fact," he said, "it could change entire complexion of ssituation. Hikop alone iss ressponsible for thiss idiocy. If he were removed...!"

Books by Keith Laumer

The Best of Keith Laumer
Fat Chance
Retief and the Warlords
Retief of the CDT
Retief's War

Published by POCKET BOOKS

Keith Laumer

RETIEF AND
THE WARLORDS

PUBLISHED BY POCKET BOOKS NEW YORK

POCKET BOOKS, a Simon & Schuster division of
GULF & WESTERN CORPORATION
1230 Avenue of the Americas, New York, N.Y. 10020

Copyright © 1968 by Keith Laumer

Published by arrangement with Doubleday & Company, Inc.
Library of Congress Catalog Card Number: 68-27128

ISBN: 0-671-81864-3

First Pocket Books printing September, 1978

10   9   8   7   6   5   4   3   2

Trademarks registered in the United States and other countries.

Printed in the U.S.A.

RETIEF AND THE WARLORDS

1

In his office on the two hundred and seventy-fifth floor of the stainless steel tower housing Sector Headquarters of the Corps Diplomatique Terrestrienne, Career Minister Magnan, Assistant Deputy Undersecretary for Inter-species Affairs, leaned back behind his twelve-foot iridium alloy desk and inspected his fingernails complacently.

"I suppose you've heard the news, Retief?" he inquired in an overly casual tone.

First Secretary Retief sent a ring of chartreuse dope-stick smoke toward a handsomely framed larger-than-life portrait of Chief of Mission Barnshingle artfully fashioned *en mosaic* from tiny chips of Yalcan glass, faithfully representing each ambassadorial skin blemish and oversized pore.

"I've heard Terran pirates are still operating here in the cluster," Retief said. "And there've been a couple of new complaints from Terry settlers of Haterakans muscling-in on the frontier worlds. But instinct tells me you have something more momentous in mind."

Magnan waved Retief's words away. "I was referring," he sniffed, "to my new assignment. Let me tell you there was a bit of jockeying for the plum among the senior staff; but in the end it was I who carried off the prize."

"What is it?" Retief inquired interestedly. "Liquor inventory?"

"I had hoped you'd greet my announcement with the solemnity appropriate to the importance of the matter." Magnan's stern look gave way to one of resignation. "But I suppose that's asking too much."

"The suspense is insupportable," Retief said. "Tell me quick."

"I," Magnan intoned impressively, "am to head up the Panel for Alien Uplift, Protection, Enlightenment, and Relief!" At Retief's inquiring look, he amplified: "The new panel will supersede the Special Unit for Conferring Knowledge on Emergent Races, as well as the Council for Humane Understanding of Minority Problems. With CHUMP and SUCKER no longer muddying the waters of inter-species togetherness, the way will be cleared for PAUPER to bestow largess on a scale hitherto undreamed of!"

"How about an organization for the benefit of Terrans?" Retief inquired. "Has anybody thought of that?"

"Hmmm; a novel notion. However, it's out of tune with the times. I wouldn't mention it if I were you. The Undersecretary takes a dim view of radicals." Magnan straightened the geometrically arranged papers on the desk before him. "After considerable thought, Retief, I've decided to allow you to volunteer as my Number Two. No"—he held up a hand—"don't thank me—"

"I wasn't going to, Mr. Magnan," Retief said. "As a matter of fact, I've been thinking about tendering my resignation, and this seems like as good a time as any—"

"But you can't!" Magnan clawed at his desk for support. "My whole scheme—that is to say, your duty . . . " He spun his Hip-U-Matic contour chair, causing the power swivel mechanism to whine in protest, flipped a switch. "Here, Retief: just let me give you a quick run-down on the state of affairs, and you'll perceive the gravity of the situation, alien-aid wise!"

A system triagram appeared in the six-foot star-tank at the

side of the room: a spherical array of bright points like a luminous popcorn ball suspended in blackness.

"Here we have the Goober Cluster," Magnan said, "with our headquarters located here." He poked a button and a tiny blue light appeared at one edge of the globe of stars. "Now, we Terrans were late-comers to the Cluster, of course. The Haterakans had already established a firm foothold in the Southern portion." He flipped a key and scattering of points around one side of the spherical cluster gleamed pink. "And here you see the Terran-occupied worlds." Magnan caused a second group of stars to glow a vivid green, in a pattern roughly opposing the pink worlds of the Haterakans.

"To date, all efforts to establish diplomatic relations with the Haterakans have come to naught," he said soberly. "The last envoy we dispatched returned coated with a substance remarkably similar to tar, to which adhered a layer of what appeared to be feathers of some sort." Magnan faced Retief solemnly. "You appreciate the implications of the contretemps?" he said expectantly.

"It suggests that the next Terry who wanders over the line had better be liberally coated with vaseline," Retief offered.

Magnan looked triumphant. "It's obvious that conditions are ripe for a PAUPER program of unprecedented proportions," he stated dramatically. "Think of it! Dozens of worlds, populated by these poor, benighted aliens, all struggling, vainly no doubt, to wrest a livelihood from the inhospitable soil, yearning for a helping hand—"

"Still, they seem to have enough resources left over from the struggle to pick fights with Terran settlers," Retief commented.

"Mere chauvinistic rumor-mongering," Magnan sniffed. "Now, as I see it, this is our opportunity to get PAUPER off the ground with a splash! What a feather in my cap, Retief, if I can secure Haterakan participation in the program! Heavens! It will be the making of me—and incidentally put an end to any incipient strife in the cluster!"

There was a harsh burp from the desk phone. Magnan turned to it in irritation as an angular female face set in an expression of permanent martyrdom popped into unflattering clarity on the screen.

"Yes, what is it, Grusona?" Magnan's mouth twitched into

the grimace of synthetic affability necessary to forstall a secretarial report of superviosry brutality.

"That creepy little Gruck, Fish or Filth or whatever his name is, wants to talk to you," the apparition announced in a voice like a meat saw encountering bone.

"The name of the Groaci Ambassador happens to be Fiss," Magnan corrected sternly. " You may inform His Excellancy

"I'll put him on," Grusona snapped, and blanked the screen. The pale, five-eyed face of the alien diplomat appeared.

"See here, Magnan," the Groaci began abruptly, "I have just been apprised by neutral sources of a new attack by imperialistic Terrestrial bandits on the inoffensive persons of a party of picnicking Haterakans—"

"Ah-ah—manners, manners." Magnan held up an admonitory hand. "I don't believe I saw so much as a courteous click of the mandibles before you launched your tirade, my dear Fiss. After all, we must preserve the amenities, eh?"

"Out upon the amenities!" Fiss hissed, vibrating his throat sac in a distressed way. "Once more the innocent lie in windrows, massacred by unprincipled warmongering Terran colonialists!"

"Surely you exaggerate." Magnan's mouth twitched in annoyance. "My report states that a small interworld barge shooed off a Haterakan vessel intruding in Terran-occupied space—"

"I warn you," Fiss whispered, "the Groacian Autonomy can not longer endure in silence—"

"Silence?" Magnan sniffed. "You've been ringing me up daily with your ridiculous little tattlings. Why don't you just send along a bill for reparations as usual and spare a scene?" He switched off the furious alien in mid-riposte.

"I confess I'm growing a trifle weary of Fiss's importunities," he said. "On the other hand, these freebooters *are* an embarrassment to Terran policy in the cluster. While you're out there, I suggest you do something about them, as well—"

"Sorry, Mr. Magnan," Retief interposed. "You got a little ahead of me there. While I'm out where?"

"Oh, didn't I tell you?" Magnan inquired brightly. "I'm sending you along to complete the arrangements for initiating the program. Now, I've already done most of the work." He lifted a thick parchment, liberally red-taped and waxsealed. "The treaty runs to ten articles, seventy-one sections, and two hundred and five individual clauses, plus codicils, amendments, riders and attachments. Something of a tour de force, if I do say so myself." He placed the heavy document before Retief. "Now, you need only secure the Haterakan signatures a mere detail and I'm as good as confirmed as a full Deputy Undersecretary."

"I'm not sure I'm ready to sprout feathers just yet," Retief said.

"Now, now." Magnan placed his fingertips together and assumed a roguish expression. "No point in leaping ahead to negative possibilities. Just think of the voyage out, via luxury liner—at Corps expense, mind you—and on per diem at that." Magnan punched buttons on his desk reference catalog. "The *Empress of Araby* sails tonight, bound for the border worlds . . ."

Half an hour later, Magnan concluded his briefing. "Now," he said, glancing at his fingerwatch, "I suppose you'll want to nip over to the library and skim through a few selected reels of the statistical digests before take-off time. And while you're there, would you mind having them stat up a few hundred thousand copies of the latest mail-order catalogs? I want to ship them out to underprivileged Haterakan worlds so that they can get started picking out what they want."

As Retief rose to depart, the phone beeped raucously again. "A person insists on seeing you," Grusona barked loudly. "He—"

"Yes, yes, Grusona." Magnan winced and hastily tuned the volume down. "All in good time. After lunch, possibly, or perhaps one morning next week—"

"He says you'll see him now, if he has to tear the door down!"

"So?" Magnan's eyebrows arched. "Well, I'm hardly one to be intimidated by threats—"

There was a rending crash from the door; the panel bulged, split, and burst inward. A large, bearded man in a blue jacket, peaked cap, and leather pants tossed the doorknob aside and stooped under the sagging frame.

"If I would of knowed you was busy, I wouldn't of came," he advanced across the room, placed two fists the size of ham hocks on the Undersecretary's desk and leaned on them. "But seeing I'm here, let's you and me have a talk, O.K., Mister?"

"Why, ah, just what I was going to suggest," Magnan found his voice. "Please take a seat, Mr. ah...?"

"Bludgin; Captain Gus Bludgin of the *Warthog II,* twenty-nine days out o' Blackstrap with a cargo o' rum." The caller hoisted a massive thigh onto the corner of the desk. "Now, Mac, what I want to know is, what are you Jaspers doing about these here Hatrack gunboats! Them tin-plated crawfish have set themselfs up a tender station right on our number two moon—ran off some of our boys doing a little water mining out there and taken the place over lock, stock and distillation tanks! From there, they're swarming all over the trade lanes like cooties at a fo'castle shakedown!"

"Cooties?" Magnan squeaked. "Why, ah, I believe if you'll just have a word with the Pest Control people across the hall—"

"I'm talking about bushwhackers!" Bludgin bellowed. "The two-faced devils even took a shot at me, a good parsec and a half inside Terry territory!"

"There must be some mistake, Mr. Bluggins." Magnan hooked a finger in his collar and shot a desperate look past his visitor at Retief, who smiled encouragingly and blew a smoke ring toward the ceiling.

"The name's Bludgin, I told you, Sol!" the large man said. "And you're durn right they's a mistake, if you think I'm taking this setting down! I'm having a pair of 10 mm. Hellbores mounted in *Warthog's* stern, and the next one o'them lousy claim-jumping Lobsters I see, I blast him, no questions asked!"

"Now, now, no racial epithets," Magnan said sharply, wagging a finger at Bludgin. "Remember, aliens are just our friends we haven't met yet."

"Well, I ain't met one that's a friend o' mine," Bludgin roared. "What are you, some kind o'renegade Terry?"

"I happen to be head of PAUPER," Magnan said stiffly, and—

"Yeah?" Gus cut him off, eyeing the First Secretary's vermillion cutaway and glare-jewel cuff links. "Fer a feller with no dough you sure got fancy shore clothes. But skip that. What I want is a CDT escort to blast them lousy aliens right back to their end o' the cluster!"

Magnan gasped. "Really, Mr. Boggett, your reactionary attitudes do you small credit! Why, I wouldn't be surprised to learn that these Terran pirates we've been hearing of were responsible for the attack, and not aliens at all!"

"You nuts?" Gus inquired, squinting his boar's eyes down to red-rimmed pinpoints. "The raiders ain't interested in short-haul tramps. All they ever hit is the big passenger jobs!"

"Eh?" Magnan shot Bludgin a sharp look. "How do you happen to know that, Mr. Bludgin?"

"On account of my cousin Averill—I mean," the captain caught himself, "I, uh, heard from the boys—er . . ." He cleared his throat. "Rumors," he said. " Now let's get back to how we're gonna blast them pesky aliens—"

"*Mister* Bludget!" Magnan rose to his full height, stared upward into his visitor's unshaven face. "One more of your inflammatory anti-extra-Terrestrial outbursts, and I shall take steps which will astonish you!"

"Huh?" Bludgin eased his bulk from the desk and blinked at the aroused diplomat. "Geeze, Mister, I didn't mean—"

"Mister Magnan knows what you meant, Gus," Retief said. "That's what annoys him." He rose, put a hand under the captain's elbow and eased him toward the door. "I have a few hours to kill. Why don't you and I go along and have a quiet drink or two together?"

"Yeah—O.K." Gus ducked his head at Magnan. "But, uh, what about the Lobsters?"

"You may be sure that the Corps Diplomatique Terrestrienne has the situation well in hand, sir," Magnan said stiffly. "As a matter of fact, Retief," he added in a lower tone after the captain had passed through the door, "between Terran freebooters and certain misguided aliens, travel in the cluster is becoming impossible! And with hotheads of the captain's type spoiling for trouble, it's more vital than ever that we act with speed in implementing Operation PAUPER. I trust that, keeping in mind the vast importance of your mission, you'll leave no stone unturned in the quest for alien friendship."

"I'm not sure we'll find what we want under a rock," Retief replied. "Still, I'll do my best."

In the hall, he joined the captain. "Now, Gus," he said as they moved off toward the bar, "I'd like to hear all about your cousin Averill before my ship lifts off. . . ."

2

"It's been a most uneventful voyage, Mr. Retief." Captain MacWivery of the million-ton liner *Empress of Araby* shook his head as the barman raised an interrogatory eyebrow. "Our next port of call will be Red Eye, the end of the line, and we haven't seen a sign of the rascals—Terran *or* Haterakan."

"Still, the trip hasn't been without its compensations." Retief rose as a shapely ash-blonde in a form-hugging platinum-mesh gown approached across the room.

"Hi, there," she said breathlessly. "Mind if I join you?"

"I've got to be getting back to the bridge." MacWivery bowed and departed.

"Poor old McQuivery," the girl said. "Is he still nervous about those silly pirates?"

A lean, elderly gentleman at the next table, immaculately dressed but with his tie slightly askew, leaned closer. "Not so silly, Sally: he's solely responsible; his record could be sullied by a sudden sally."

"But meanwhile, he needn't shilly-shally, Colonel Shelley,"

14

Sally came back promptly. She turned to Retief. "I looked for you at the masquerade last night. I came as a cake of soap; all I had on was a little lavender perfume."

"I was there," Retief said, "disguised as a section of wallpaper. You were leaning on me when you told the story about the mermaid and the octopus."

"Why, I never—" She broke off as a faint but distinct tremor ran through the deck.

"What in the world was that?" She frowned.

A second shock rattled the glasses on the table.

"If I didn't know better," the colonel said to no one in particular, "I'd swear that was gunfire."

"That was our stern battery letting go with a salvo," Retief said, rising.

"But—" Sally looked alarmed. "I thought we only carried those guns as a ... a sort of decoration!"

"I'm afraid that's about all they're good for." Retief was listening intently; glanced at his watch as a third, lesser jar *crump!*ed distantly. Excited voices rang across the wide dining salon.

"By jove, that was a gun!" the colonel exclaimed.

"Port emplacement," Retief said. "One six-millimeter. They must be overhauling us in a hurry."

"You mean—*pirates?*"

"It looks that way. I have a hunch there'll be a run on the elevators in a few minutes. We may as well start now."

Anxious voices were calling up and down the corridor as the trio made their way to the nearest lift. Distant sounds were audible over the hubbub, followed by another solid vibration.

"They've put a line across us," Retief said as a faint metalic clatter was audible. "They'll be locking onto us in a few seconds."

"You mean—they're going to board us?" Sally gasped.

"Uh-huh. Just a small party. Don't worry; they won't bother the passengers."

Abruptly, a crackle came from the PA annunciator overhead.

"Attention, all passengers and crew," a voice with only a slight quaver said, "All passengers will report at once to the main lounge, First Class, B Deck aft. All crew with the exception of stand-by Power Section personnel will also report to main lounge . . ." He stumbled over several words as he repeated the announcement.

"It's a raid, all right," Retief said. "I understand they work on a tight routine. They'll have studied the plans of the ship, and won't waste a move. This whole operation won't take twenty minutes. You'd better go along to the lounge now. Rumor has it that late arrivals annoy them."

"What are *you* going to do?" Sally gasped.

"I'm going to see if I can't introduce a couple of small variations into the routine." Retief turned and made his way off quickly through the crowd.

2

The mob of excited passengers filled the passage, making Retief's upstream progress difficult. A harassed ship's officer spied him, called out sharply, "Here, fellow, the lounge is in this direction!"

"Just going back for my hearing aid," Retief called cheerfully, and forged on. At the intersecting cross-corridor, he turned left, toward the ship's port side. The amber light of a service lift glowed ahead. He rode it down six levels, left it at K deck, followed a narrower corridor back past empty administrative offices. He paused at a sound of boots ahead, stepped into a darkened storeroom, watched a party of raiders approach: five rough-and-ready types in rumpled gray shipsuits, led by a lanky, sharp-eyed, big nosed man with a military-type side arm and metal shoulder tabs that might have been insignia of rank. When they had passed, Retief went on, bypassed the Power Section, cut through a stacked cargo hold, emerged in a dim-lit 'tweendecks loft devoted to lifeboat equipment. Directly below, he knew from his study of the vessel's layout, was the Boarding Hold, opening onto the main entry lock. The ship was strangely silent now. Retief moved quietly across to the companionway hatch, knelt and put his ear to it, heard a faint mutter of voices.

Beside the hatch was a manual crank for emergency operation. He gave the latter a careful three turns, opening a quarter-inch space which gave him a view of a stretch of gray decking, the inner lock doors, standing open, and two men, both husky, heavy-jawed, one young, one middle-aged. The former carried a late-model crater gun cradled in the crook of his arm. The other fingered the stock of a 3 mm. blast rifle.

". . . too close," the youngster was muttering worriedly. "One o' these times Lou's going to slice it too thin."

"What's it to us?" The other worked loose lips and spat wetly on the immaculate deck. "You know the orders. Anything goes haywire topside, we cut out fast."

"And leave Lou and the boys behind—" The youngster broke off, lifted a communicator strapped to the underside of his thick wrist, listened, frowning.

"Fifteen seconds ahead of schedule," he told the other man.

"So what? They still got fifteen minutes to louse it up in."

"Fourteen."

Retief eased away from the hatch, rose and moved silently across the loft, ducked through an undersized communicating door. In the gloom, the dark shape of a ventilator manifold loomed among shadows. He took a flat case from his pocket, opened it and extracted a tiny cylinder, gave it a sharp twist, inserted it in the access hole on the side of the housing. Then he returned to the hatch.

A minute passed. The two men below talked in nervous mutters. The younger man raised his head and sniffed.

"Hey, Ben," he said. "Smells like something's burning!"

"Calm down," the other said. "You're smelling things."

"No, I'm not—they're pulling something!" The younger man's voice was tight. "Maybe I better tip Lou—" His hand moved to his communicator.

"Nix," his partner cut in. "I'll go take a look around; you cover here and keep your eyes open." He moved off. Retief waited fifteen seconds, then cranked the hatch open another half inch, slipped a small, slim-barreled gun from under his left arm, took careful aim at the back of the neck of the man below, and pressed the trigger. There was a soft *zik!* The man slapped at his neck with a muffled curse, then stood, swaying slightly. The gun slipped from his hands, swung dangling from its sling. Retief pressed the switch to cycle the hatch wide, slid through, dropped softly to the deck. The sentry stood flat-footed, staring vaguely into a corner. Retief looked along the passage. The other man was not in sight.

"Eighteen seconds ahead of schedule," a tiny voice rasped

from the comm unit at the boarder's wrist. *"Twelve minutes and counting."* Retief walked past the man into the lock. The red safety light glowed inside the open entry valve of the raiders' jolly boat. He paused for a moment to play a pocket detector beam around the port and over the floor inside. There was no *ping!* warning of a trap. He stepped through.

It was a small boat, a standard Concordiat Naval model scout. Retief went quickly forward along an equipment-packed passage into the cramped command deck. At the navigator's panel, he used a tool to remove a small access cover, took a quarter-inch cube of opaque plastic from the case in his pocket, carefully crimped the four silvery leadout wires to four contacts in the heart of the apparatus. He replaced the pane, went back to the lock.

In the corridor the young sentry was standing as he had left him. The other man was still out of sight along the curve of the passage. Retief stepped close to the doped man.

"What's your name?" He put the question in a low tone.

"Jack. Jack Raskall," the man said dully.

"Look at me, Jack."

The man turned vacant eyes on him. "Listen carefully, Jack. The key word is 'talisman.' When you hear that word you'll recognize me as Bully West, your old pal from back home. Understand?"

"Bull West...old pal...back home," the man muttered.

"By the way, where is 'back home'?" Retief asked.

"Back home...on Outpost. Broken Bone...great little town. Home..."

"Swell, Jack. Now forget I talked to you. You've been standing here waiting for Ben. You haven't seen a thing." Retief turned, jumped for the hatch, pulled himself up and in. As the cover circled shut, he heard feet approaching.

"Nothing," Ben said as he came up. "Anything here?"

"I just been standing here waiting for you," the other said indifferently. "I haven't seen a thing."

3

"You were right, Retief," the ship's captain said fifteen minutes later, mopping at his neck with a king-size tissue bearing the ornate symbol of the Ten Planet Line. "They knew exactly what they were doing; walked straight to the strong room and cut the safe out of the vault with fission saws. Didn't look at anything else, didn't molest anyone except the assistant purser; knocked him tail over tea kettle when he made a move toward the interlock. Got away clean with a CDT payroll of three-quarters of a million in Bank of New Brooklyn tapes. Took them just under twenty minutes for the whole show."

"Now it's our turn to put a little salt on their tails," Retief said. He followed the captain through a lock onto the boat deck. The latter indicated a blunt shape resting in Number One Bay, from which four nattily uniformed crewmen were peeling back a tarpaulin to reveal a one-man space gig, scarred and pittied from stem to stern tubes.

"There she is, Mr. Retief—rigged to your specifications precisely," the captain said. "Very tricky, mutilating her in such a way as to appear to almost totally demolish her, and at the same time leave her more or less spaceworthy." He held out his hand. "It's a damn fool stunt—but maybe it will pay off. Nothing else has."

Retief stepped up on the heat-blasted hull, slipped in under the precisely warped hatch. Settled in the scorched acceleration chair, he glanced over the carefully cracked dials of the instrument, then pressed the RELEASE button. Machinery hummed. Seconds later he felt the sudden lift and surge as the mother ship's launcher tossed the boat out into the emptiness of interstellar space. He lined up on the faint signal from the telltale he had planted in the corsair's navigation computer, set his controls on FULL CRUISE and settled down for the chase.

4

For the next five hours the fleeing pirate set a pace that held the finely tuned power unit of the gig at maximum acceleration to retain the tiny blip on-screen, almost lost in the fierce blaze from a dozen G-type suns within half a light-year. Extrapolating from the course line, Retief concluded that the corsairs were headed for a small world listed in the catalog as Blue Moon.

He unstrapped from the cramped chair, opened the wall locker and took out a well-worn shipsuit of dark blue polyon, a pair of expensive-looking but battered ship boots, a short military jacket from which insignia had been carelessly cut, and a gun belt and holster with a power pistol of antique design which had been carefully modified by an unlicensed armorer in an unsavory side street in Oldport. He donned the outfit, fed his discarded clothes into the waste converter, then punched a packaged dinner of *entrecôte* and black Bacchus wine. As he finished the meal, there was a sharp *ping!* from the screen.

The bright point that was the racing pirate was no longer alone. From the concealment of an obscuring finger of gas, another blip had appeared, accelerating on a converging course with the lone ship.

"Well," Retief murmured. "A welcoming committee..." He advanced the drive to FULL GATE, watched as the lining temperatures climbed past 3000° C.

On the screen, the newcomer was rapidly closing the gap. At a million miles, the pirate, apparently just sensing the new arrival, abruptly changed course in a bone-breaking maneuver. The intercepting craft leaped foward; the readout windows beside Retief's screen indicated a 10-G acceleration—enough to overload any standard antiac installation. The pirate surged ahead at full drive, altered course again in a swerving evasion pattern. Now the minute pinpricks of missiles were visible, lancing outward from the interceptor. One disappeared in a tiny flare; a second winked and was gone. The third was no more than half a second from target when it detonated.

Retief flipped levers on his panel, cutting the drive and throwing power to the specially devised signal-suppressor gear which would render his tiny craft invisible to all but the most acute sensors. Far ahead, the chase craft now paced the pirate vessel, inexorably narrowing the gap between itself and its quarry to a thousand miles, eight hundred, five hundred—

Without warning, the hard-pressed corsair veered toward its tormentor. In an instant, the gap had closed to a hundred miles—and in that instant, a flight of six bright sparks arched out toward the stranger. Four brilliant detonations flashed almost as one as the interceptor picked off the attackers; a fifth flared in the next second—and then the sixth, so close that on Retief's screens it had seemed to merge with its target.

The next seconds seemed to confirm the hit. The aggressor lagged, its course diverging now at a no-G velocity as its intended victim swung away on a flat course. Then, just as it appeared its prey would escape, the stranger steadied suddenly and launched a projectile directly at the stern of the fleeing ship.

"Right up the tail pipe," Retief said aloud. The screens flashed and darkened, filtering out the sunlike glare of the detonating missile. A full minute passed before the view resolved into a churning vortex of expanding luminosity in which subcenters of violence boiled and glowed as the ravening energy bomb fed on the fragments of its kill. The prow of the stricken pirate vessel appeared from the glowing cloud, trailing wreckage; two-thirds of the ship's length had been blasted away. The surviving fragment rotated slowly, strewing its contents in a widening spiral on which the light of the surrounding stars winked and glimmered. Far off to one side, the attacking vessel hurtled on aimlessly on a ballistic course. Retief watched closely, but no lifeboat appeared from the shattered wreck. He corrected course, and at low power setting, moved in toward the scene of the disaster.

5

Retief watched the derelict swell on his forward screen as he came up in the cone of shadow cast by the nearest major star. At five miles, he shut down all power, switched his scanners to high mag and studied the wreckage for signs of life. Small puffs of vapor were visible jetting from the ripped-open end of the truncated vessel, indicating that she was still holding some atomosphere behind a partially sealed bulkhead. He drifted in close, used a touch of power to edge in among the twisted structural members arching up in a ragged ring surrounding the black interior. He clamped the boat to a broken girder, pulled on a vacuum suit and helmet, valved his lock open and kicked out into the blaze of starlight.

His suit light gleamed on warped and torn hull plating, massive keel members curled and snapped like taffy by the heat of the explosion and still radiating enough heat to make his suit's cooling system labor. There were snarls of conduit and piping, melted into spaghetti-like globs. Flotsam from the Power Section, the storage holds, the crew quarters drifted among the black-gleaming ball bearings of all sizes that were solidified lumps of the metal that had flowed like water half an hour before.

And scattered like bright confetti through the ruins, gold, iridium, and platinum coins drifted—loot from raided vaults.

Retief maneuvered carefully among the sharp-edged wreckage, found the open end of what had been the axial passage typical of the old Naval Arm ships. A dead man drifted a few yards inside it, his suit blackened and charred, the faceplate collapsed. Retief pushed past the corpse, picked his way forward, warding off floating rubbish. He reached the forward vacuum lock, almost invisible in the haze of ice crystals forming from the gas leaking around the warped seals. It swung inward at a shove; the inside pressure was almost gone. He cycled the inner door, and was in a passage that looked almost normal, even to the dim radiance of the emergency lighting strip along the ceiling.

Ten feet ahead a closed door lettered COMMAND DECK—AUTHORIZED PERSONNEL ONLY blocked his progress. He tried the entry switch; there was a metallic clacking sound from beyond the panel, and the lights dimmed down to a wavering glow. Retief unholstered the power gun at his hip, set it at needlebeam, and burned through the lock mechanism. He shoved the door open and stepped into the room beyond.

Broken glass hung in the air, glittering like the shards of a blasted glacier. Smoke still wafted from the blackened interiors of the fire-gutted panels. Four men, all wearing vacuum suits, hung slack in their acceleration harnesses. Retief went to the nearest man slumped over the shattered chart table. He was dead, his suit ripped, frozen blood caked ruby red inside the faceplate. The next man was the one called Ben, also dead. Retief checked the third, found a faint pulse. The last of the four was the tall, big-nosed man he had seen leading the boarding party; he was alive, with blood on his face.

There were emergency oxygen tanks at one side of the circular deck. Retief pounded the control valve and gas hissed out in a frosty jet. He patched wires, fed a trickle of power into the stand-by heating units. In five minutes the temperature had risen to a bearable level; the atmospheric pressure leveled off at 9 psi, though the chamber was still losing gas through the broken lock seal.

Retief unlocked the big-nosed man's helmet, lifted it off. He stirred and groaned. His eyes opened, stared vaguely, then fixed, with difficulty, on Retief.

"Who're you?" he said blurrily, and made a move to unlock his harness. Retief put out a hand to steady him as he wavered to his feet, but the man knocked it away clumsily.

"Out of my way," he croaked, and took a stumbling step, caught at the next chair for support.

"The navigator's dead." Retief took the big-nosed man's upper arm in a firm grip. "So's Ben. The other man's still breathing."

The big-nosed man swung at him feebly. Retief *tsked* and eased him back to the couch.

"Better calm down, Lou," he said. "You're still in plenty of trouble. We're losing pressure fast, and the reserve tanks won't last long. And by the way," he added as the man's eyes swept the ruined panels, "the rear three-quarters of your command is missing, so don't count on going anywhere for a while."

"What . . . you mean?" The man started out of the couch and Retief pushed him back casually.

"Who were they, Lou? Old friends of yours? I noticed you peeled off in a hurry as soon as you sighted them."

The close-set black eyes squinted in a ferocious frown.

"What are you, a joker?" the man snarled. "You ought to be an expert on 'em. You tell *me* who they are!"

Retief shook his head. "Sorry, Lou. I didn't get much of a look at them.'"

"Where are they? Waiting outside for you to soften me up? They think I'll fold up and cry on their shoulder if their Judas goat throws his hat in first?"

"You lost me on that one, Lou." Retief turned to the second survivor. The man's face was invisible behind the fogged faceplate. He reached for the release lever and behind him the big-nosed man's voice barked: "Don't touch him!"

Retief turned. There was a deadly-looking blast gun in Lou's hand, aimed at his head.

"I could have scrambled you where you stood, but first I wanted to hear you tell it, big boy," Lou grated. "How'd they get to you? What are they paying you that makes it worth it?"

"You seem to have gotten hold of a couple of false impressions, Lou," Retief said easily. "I arrived on the scene a few minutes after the blowup, and came over on the off-chance somebody had lived through it."

"Sure you did," Lou said between gritted teeth. "I should have known better than to waste time on you. Say a prayer if you know one, turncoat..." He pushed the gun forward, grinning a fierce grin—

"hey...Lou..." a weak voice spoke up. Both men turned. The second survivor was tugging at his helmet. "What happened? We were clear...?"

"Not quite," Lous grated. "But I'm taking one rat with us..."

The helmet came up, and the face that had been behind it   a battered visage with one eye swollen shut and blood on the chin from a split lip—swung to Retief.

"Talisman," the latter said softly.

"Bully...Bully West!" the man blurted. "What in the name of the little devils in Hellport are *you* doing here?"

"You know this bimbo?" Lou's hand jerked.

"He's my pal! Good old Bully! We're from the same town, Broken Bone, back on Outpost!"

"Well, your old pal's made new friends since you saw him. He's with *them*."

Jack Raskall's jaw dropped. "Huh? Lou, you're nuts! Bull West is the greatest guy that ever lived! He's true-blue! He wouldn't sell out to no Hatracks—not Bull West!"

"I'm supposed to believe he was just joy riding in the neighborhood—six million miles in deep space? Hah! I don't take stock in that kind of coincidence!" Lou said, but the gun was aimed off side now. He glanced at Raskall. "How are you, Jack? Can you walk?"

"I...I guess I'm O.K." Jack's eyes went to the still bodies hanging in their harnesses.

"How about Sammy and Dingo and   "

"They didn't have a chance." Lou motioned with the gun. "Let's take a slant at your boat, Mister."

"Better button up. The air's thin out there." Retief unsealed the lock and the men pushed through as air whistled into the passage. The outer part swung open on tangled wreckage and raw space; Lou stared, cursed in a hard monotone. Retief pointed to the small, battered gig clamped to the arching rib. Lou grunted.

"Huh. Couldn't tell it from the rest of the junk." He pushed forward, studied the boat in the gleam from his suit light. "What happened? You claim they shot you up, too?"

"Whatta you think?" Jack Raskall spoke up. "He had it built special? Use your head, Lou! Good old Bull West is in the same fix as us. Let's start thinking about how we're going to get out of this."

"Your boat's still operational, eh?" Lou demanded.

"That's right," Retief agreed. "But she won't carry all of us."

"Jack'll go." The big-nosed man eyed Retief. "He'll make the run in and bring out a relief party. Any objections?"

"None on my part," Retief said mildly. "But..."

"But what?" Lou barked and the gun in his hand jumped up.

"*They* might have something to say about it." Retief looked past Lou. The dark man turned, froze. High on a blackened rib projecting above them, a figure moved, silhouetted against the clotted stars of cluster. Fierce, oversized eyes glinted down at the three men through a bulbous air-helmet. Behind the alien, a second and third appeared, and more, perched all around the rim of the shattered hull. With a snarl, the man called Lou brought up the gun—and Retief slammed a blow to his wrist, knocked the weapon spinning away into darkness.

"Make no other move, ssavage Terriess," a harsh, croaking voice rasped in their headsets. "You are property of Fleetmaster Harrumph now, and for moment it iss hiss pleasure that you live."

3

Retief and his two fellow prisoners stood on the crumpled hull-plates, guarded by half a dozen aliens, each of whom was armed with a weapon resembling a bright-metal javelin ornamented with knobs and levers. The creatures were impossibly tall, spider-lean, bristling with quills. In the starlight, their horny hides, the color of a boiled crustacean, gleamed with a dull metallic luster. Two of their four arms were mounted just below the bony neck, the elbows projecting vertically upwards, ending in a pair of six-inch crabclaws. The lower pair, articulated horizontally and equipped with fingers like clumps of pink worms, held the weapons. There were four legs, two stout-thighed, lean-shinned, cased in polished greaves, two smaller, mounted posteriorly, supporting the rear section of the segmented body. Across the tops of their bullet heads, a single ridge swept backward to form a spikelike horn. Below, a pair of thorned hooks depended, framing the mouth. No clothing was apparent, but all were vividly ornamented with paint in geometric patterns on their bodies. Behind them, their long, slim vessel hung motionless a hundred yards away, glinting in the dazzle of starlight like a hundred-yard-long fountain pen, marred amidships by a ragged puncture from which dim, greenish light glowed.

"Plugged by a two-bit slinghot like that," Lou grunted disgustedly. "And sold out—twice—by a turncoat." He gave Retief a vicious look.

"Aw, for Grunt's sake, Lou," Jack spoke up. "Bull's in this just like us, ain't he? He's got a gun aimed at his gizzard too—"

"I said forget it!"

"Listen, Bully," Jack said. "We don't know much about these Hatracks. Damn few Terries have ever seen one to talk about it—"

"Shut up, Jack!" Lou snapped. "Don't spill your guts to this spy!"

"No more jabber, untamed oness," a Haterakan voice cut into the conversation. "Ssledss arrive now to take you to your confinement."

The vehicles that came up, snorting pale jets of bluish fire, were nothing more than twenty-foot poles with saddles mounted along them. The Terrans climbed up, took their places, with Haterakan guards between them; the shuttles wafted them across to the alien ship. They entered through a narrow slit in the sharply curved hull.

"Remove your falsse skinss!" a guard ordered, and made a threatening gesture with his gun.

Retief's analyzer gauge indicated breathable air; he flipped his helmet open. Beside him, Lou snorted.

"Phooie! Smells like a fox farm in here."

"Be glad your smeller's got something to work on," Jack said as he pulled off his vacuum suit. "I got three minutes' suit air left."

The guards motioned them along an alley-like corridor, paused before a high, heavily embossed door, and after an exchange of barked formalities, motioned the captives inside.

It was a wide, high room, with a curving wall that tapered up to a massive bull's-eye of black glass from which a chandelier of metal hooks and baubles hung, glittering with an eye-dazzling glare. Behind an elaborate construction of polished metal bars, an alien perched at ease in a hammock-like arrangement of tooled blue leather set with silver knobs, fingering a captured

Terran pistol with boneless digits. His headplates, wider-flaring than those of his subordinates, were polished to a steely glitter, topped with an ornamental spike from which a cluster of violet plumes sprang. His chest, as hard and bright as the cuirass of a conquistador, bore loops of gold wire and boldly stenciled patterns of red and yellow and blue and white enamel. He wore a chin-strapped pillbox cap; an elaborately tailored short jacket with heavy braided epaulets fitted his complicated double shoulders like a second hide, completing the portrait of martial splendor. The alien swiveled his immense eyes at his guests, rasped his shredding hooks to produce a nerve-racking sound.

"Live sspecimehss," he said in a voice like a defective servomotor. "Excellent!" He motioned with an upper arm and the guards withdrew. "I am Master of Fleets Harrumph," he continued. "I ssuppose you are wondering why I trouble with you, eh?"

"Nuts," Lou said.

The Haterakan casually bent the duraloy barrel of the power gun into a U, tossed it aside, picked up a silvery wand. He twisted it, sliding telescoping sections in and out, peering at it like an engineer using a slide rule.

"Ah, here we are. Nutss, berriess, sseedss, grainss . . . You are hungry, yess? Very well, there will be slopss in plenty for you, lucky beastss. And warm nesstss and many sshess."

"Many whats?" Raskall wrinkled his forehead.

The official worked the slide dictionary again. "Femaless, wenchess, petticoatss, matronss, squawss, bitchess, doess, bitss of fluff. You would like that, eh?"

"Oh boy," Jack said.

"And what do you Lobsters get out of the deal?" Lou snarled.

"Haterakan war aimss are ssimplicity itsself," the alien said reasonably. "To enrich oursselvess at Terran expensse. What elsse? As for yoursselvess—your troubless are over. You will live happily, ssecure. How many litterss can you sspawn in month, Terry?"

"Wha?"

"Don't talk to the damned thing," Lou barked.

"Ssilence, sslave!" the Fleetmaster barked peremptorily. He eyed Lou closely. "Haven't we met before?" he inquired. "Of course all you aliens look alike; still, I have feeling we've met ssocially."

"Not bloody likely," Lou spat.

"Good, I sshould disslike to ensslave a former guesst."

With a snarl, Lou started toward the Haterakan. The latter moved swiftly, but Retief was quicker; he slammed his doubled fist, with one knuckle projecting, in a short, powerful jab to the man's short ribs. Lou doubled over, sank to the floor.

"Ah, rogue, doubtless untamable." Fleetmaster Harrumph peered down at the casualty. He plucked what was obivously a gun from a jeweled shoulder holster, aimed it negligently at Lou. Retief took a step and stood straddling the fallen pirate. "It wouldn't do to dispose of him, Fleetmaster. He's vital to the harmony of our vibrations. Represents the eternal dissonance of the *sturm* versus *angst* and all that sort of thing. Without him the rest of us will get peckish, pick at our slops, and turn in a miserable performance litterwise."

"Ah, soo. Curiouss—but as for yoursself, you look forward with delight to prosspect I outlined, eh?"

"Sounds like the workingman's dream," Retief said admiringly. "When does the program get under way?"

"Soon. It remainss merely to complete certain arrangementss for the acquissition of grazing landss and ssuitable herdss—arrangements which even now near fulfillment—and then you will be released among your cowss and natural increasse will ssoon inssure contented flockss gamboling on brown! How proud you'll be to see sturdy little ones about you!"

"A charming prospect," Retief agreed. "But without our chum here, it's all a dream."

"Well, in that case, I ssupposse I musst let him carry on— but I'll hold you other two unitss sstrictly ressponssible! Any violenss, and sskorff! Into grinderss he goess."

"I heard you Hatracks killed Terries on sight," Jack spoke up. "What makes us different?"

"You, my dear creature, are ssurvivor typess—a valuable trait—as demonstrated by your pressent survival." He rasped his shredding hooks together. "You see, I confide in you, hopeful that you will be content in the cozy den I will provide aboard sship, remembering the merry outlook before you!"

"Hey," Jack Raskall muttered. "What's he talking about, Bully? Why's he interested in fixing us up with like bachelor's paradises?"

"Didn't you hear him?" Lou gasped, as the guards hauled him

to his feet. "The son of a boat hook's going to breed Terries!"

"What for?" Jack's mouth hung open.

"But what elsse?" the Haterak said in a reasonable tone. "To eat!"

2

"Now," Harrumph said genially, "there are few ssmall pointss you may clear up for me, thereby minimizing difficultiess in ssecuring your future penss and wallowss." He poked a button and a star map appeared on a wall screen.

"Here we ssee your future home, delightful little planet you are ssure to enjoy, known to its present inhabitants as Blue Moon."

"Huh?" Jack Raskall blurted.

"Don't interrupt, Jack," Retief admonished. "After all, we want to hear about our future home, don't we?"

"Now the quesstion of possible orbital defensses arissess,"Harrumph continued. As he talked, Retief moved casually closer to the desk, caught Jack's eye, tilted his head in a quick signal toward the open door, beyond which the guards waited. Jack blinked, closed his mouth, nudged Lou.

"...sso if you will jusst mention any meassuress which you feel might be useful..." The Fleetmaster produced an awesome parody of an encouraging smile.

"Uh...I can't see good." Lou moved forward, made a show of craning his neck, edging toward the desk.

"I got some hot dope to pass along, so's to cinch that swell deal you was talking about"—Jack craned his neck, moved casually to place himself beside the door—"how about shifting the map off to the left a little, where I can see better?"

Harrumph turned, reached for the knob.

"Better?" he inquired.

"Much better," Retief said—and dived across the pigeonholed desk. Harrumph emitted a startled grunt and struck out with his pincers, but Retief dodged the slashing claws, caught an upper limb in a hammer lock, wrenched it over and back. With an agonized snort, the Fleetmaster performed a neat backflip, landed on the floor with Retief astride him. Behind him, there was a rasp of feet as Jack whirled and slammed the door shut in the face of reinforcements.

Under Retief, Harrumph made a sound like a spoon in a garbage grinder, threshing all eight limbs. Retief seized one of his captive's major ankles, bent the leg back, grabbed a peg-shaped plastic stylus from the desk, set it against the knee joint, and with a sharp blow of the palm, drove it home. At the blow, the Haterakan gave a lunge, broke free, rose to assorted knees, and fell with a crash as the wedged limb failed to function. Jack vaulted the desk, landed astride the armored back as Lou swung a kick, missed, connected solidly with Raskall's jaw. As Jack sprawled, out cold, Retief jumped clear, grabbed up a weapon from the desk, motioned the Haterakan back as he tried again to rise. A vigorous pounding had started up at the door.

"We've still got the crew to handle," Lou rasped, breathing hard.

"Oh, I think the Fleetmaster will know how to deal with them," Retief replied, aiming the gun carelessly toward the incapacitated officer as he rose shakily from the floor, his plumes broken, his tunic askew, the braid torn from his collar, his jaunty cap dangling by its strap.

"Take care, sslavess," he started—and backed up hastily as Lou made a threatening move. "Former sslaves, that iss," he corrected. "As for my crew, I sshall insstruct them to return you to your former ssituation at once, as you have failed to qualify for the program—"

"No need to go to all the trouble," Retief said. "Just tell them to abandon ship."

"Abandon sship?" Harrumph drew himself up stiffly. "Never!"

"In that case—" Retief raised the weapon as Lou and Jack closed in.

"Never fear, I mean," the alien amended. "Jusst what I was going to ssuggest!" He depressed a key on his desk and croaked an order.

For the next five minutes, the three Terrans and the Haterakan hostage waited, eyeing each other in tense silence. Then there was the distant clatter of an air lock opening, followed by a series of thumps.

"Forty-nine, fifty," Harrumph counted down. "That iss all, my dear Teriress. Now, I ssupposse you musst be hurrying along...."

"Not quite," Retief said. "We'll stick together a while longer.

There are a couple of other things you'll want to do for us—just as an expression of good will."

"But—of coursse." Harrumph eyed the guns calculatingly.

"Check the corridor, Jack," Retief said.

"All clear, Bully," Raskall reported a moment later.

"We're going to the control room now, Fleetmaster,"Retief advised the alien captain. He motioned the alien ahead of him into the corridor, now silent and empty. "Better play it real pretty now," he advised. "After this asuspicious start, I wouldn't want our friendship marred by having to shoot you."

3

In the navigation room of the captured ship, Harrumph concluded his explanation of the controls.

"It iss really mosst disstressing," he growled plaintively. "I wass assured by Hikop, my Grand Admiral, that you Terriess were most docile of domesstic beasstss; and now here am I, giving piloting instructions at gunpoint to my own livestock!"

"I'm afraid the Admiral fell for our propaganda," Retief said. "We like to spring these little surprises, just to lend a spice to the formal proceedings."

Harrumph sighed heavily. "To think that I permitted myself to be sso grossly missled. Sstill, all iss not losst. Ass you ssee, the sysstem iss ssimplicity itsself. Jusst employ reassonable care and you will bring uss all ssafe to port. I ssuggest you correct coursse now; we approach patrolled territory and it would be pity to precipitate unfortunate incident."

"You're too palsy by half with that Lobster," Lou said. "He acts like he's on his way to a rest home instead of a jailhouse. I think he's got an angle up his cuff."

"The curiouss cusstomss of your Terrestrialss with regard to prissonerss of war iss well known," Harrumph pointed out. "I antissipate a resstful internment—until the arrival of my associatess, who will releasse me, after which the iron boot will be on the other foot."

Retief examined the gun he had taken from Harrumph's desk. "Odd,"he said. "This seems to be a conversion from a standard Bogan 3 mm."

Lou scowled. "Just proves I was right! Some lousy renegade Terry has been supplying these Lobsters. How about it, you?" He glared at the alien. "Where'd you get it?"

"We have our methodss," Harrumph replied haughtily. "Code of honor of Haterakan officer permitss me to ssay no more. Now, kindly forbear to pump me for information, or I'll be forced to report you to commandant of interment facility."

"Sorry to disappoint you, Fleetmaster," Retief said, studying the star chart. "But the cozy concentration camp will have to wait for more urgent business."

"What'ss this? You don't intend to take any foolissh rissks, I trusst!" Harrumph croaked in alarm.

"I'm sure that with the benefit of your advice we'll be able to avoid some of the more dangerous errors," Retief said.

"Why don't we burn him down and haul freight out of here?" Lou demanded darkly.

"Have some sense, Lou," Jack Raskall came back awkwardly through his swollen jaw. "Bully's got to pump him for all the info he can get."

Lou glowered, rubbing his bruised ribs.

"Yeah," Jack said, noting the gesture. "It's that bellyache that's graveling you. But Bully saved your neck for you when he clobbered you."

"Yeah—a cute punch. Just wait till I get *my* licks in."

"Jack, how much do you know about Blue Moon's planetary defense setup?" Retief inquired.

"Heck—not much, Bully—no more'n you, I guess."

"I trusst you contemplate no unwisse action," Harrumph croaked worriedly. "You have merely to set your coursse homeward, and *groonk!* There you are!"

"I'm afraid we'll be heading in the opposite direction," Retief said.

"What's that you said?" Lous cocked his head. "That'll take us right square into Hatrack territory!"

"Not quite; just as far as Blue Moon."

"Are you off your turnip? From what this sucker-stick says, every Hatrack in this end of the Arm will be headed that way!"

"Listen to him, Lou," Jack put in. "Bully's right—attack or no attack, you know as well as I do orders were for all of us Legion members to make that rendezvous at Blue Moon—"

"Button that lip, Raskall!" Lou caught at the younger man's arm, spun him around. "That's classified military information you're spilling!"

"Looky, Lou." Raskall jerked his arm free. "I guess I'm getting a little tired of you throwing your weight around. Lay off me, see, or I'll forget those stripes you're wearing and bend that big schnozz of yours so far out of line you can use it for an ear!"

"You and what platoon of wet-heads?" Lou gave the reference member two quick stokes with a thumb, feinted a left hook, bounced back, bobbing and weaving. Jack went into a crouch, raised his hands as though he were aiming a basketball for a free-throw from the foul line. "Yah!" he said. "Couldn't hit the broad end of a barmaid—"

"Now, gentlemen," Retief said, "maybe you'd better conserve those valuable hostilities for use on the opposition."

"I'll kill him," Lou muttered, delivering two left jabs and a snappy right cross to a volume of space two yards from Jack's head.

"Oh boy, I'll murder ya, ya bum." Jack held his elbows to his sides, faked a feint and backpedaled.

"Playtime comes later." Retief stepped between the warriors. "We have work to do now."

"Work?" Both men turned on Retief, looking indignant. He pointed to the screen, where an array of bright points had appeared ahead, on a converging course, gleaming against the stars scattered across their path. Lou swore loudly.

"That cuts it! The whole blasted Hatrack fleet, looks like, cutting square across our bows!"

"Ye gods! The place is swarming with 'em!" Jack blurted. "How come we never spotted 'em before?"

"My sship iss equipped with excellent anti-detection apparatuss," Harrumph explained blandly, "which I have but now attuned to private recognition band: thus we observe fleet with easse. Impressive, eh?"

"What about it, Bully?" Jack peered at the screen worriedly. "There must be a hundred o' them slingshots!"

"Take care now," Harrumph admonished. "This is armed patrol interdicting approachess to coming sscene of action. They will sshoot on ssight! Not only iss welfare of Fleetmaster at sstake, but you musst remember that you yourselvess are valuable livesstock, not lightly to be wassted!"

"A cogent point," Retief conceded. " I hope you'll keep it in the forefront of your thought during the coming minutes."

"What you going to do, Bully?" Jack stared into the screen on which the enemy fleet was growing rapidly closer on a converging course.

"We can't get through them, as Lou pointed out," Retief said. "So we'll join them."

"Wha—?" Lou rounded on Retief. "Why, you lousy renegade—!"

Jack took a quick step; his fist, describing a short arc, thudded home against the big-nosed man's jaw; Lou slammed to the floor face-first, lay like a corpse.

"That evens up for the boot in the kisser," Raskall said cheerfully, rubbing his fist. "I was about tired o' his yapping. Now, what was you saying, Bully?"

"We'll fall into formation and let them convoy us as long as we're all going in the same direction, They won't fire on us unless we make a false move. Harrumph, get on your fleet microband and try to raise your admiral."

Harrumph busied himself coughing and barking at the intership screen. An answering burst of snorts and gasps came back.

"All iss well sso far," the captive announced. "Admiral Hikop congratulates me on my timely arrival and orders me to take up my position."

Retief studied the enemy fleet. "These gunboats of yours are pretty small bore for taking over a planet," he commented.

"It iss known from our preliminary intelligence surveyss that frontier worldss enjoy little in way of defensess," the alien replied. "We have planned our assault accordingly."

"Maybe you'd better fill me in on the details of the attack plan," Retief suggested. "Just to avoid accidents."

"A moment, while I check on latest order of battle." There was another exchange in Haterakan, while the captive boat forged on, closing on the rearmost units of the advancing fleet. Beside Retief, Jack Raskall chewed the inside of his cheek and stared into the screens at the host of small but deadly craft that comprised the Haterakan flotilla. On the floor, Lou groaned and stirred.

Harrumph concluded his conversation and turned to Retief.

"Ssimplissity itsself," he croaked cheerfully. "We will make initial sstrike at widely separated pointss; then, when native forcess have dissperssed to oppose uss, we will foregather to establish our beachhead on major continent's northern plain."

On the screen, a tiny, glaring disk was passing off the port bow.

"That's Emporium," Jack said huskily. "Big commercial center. We're passing mighty close. Looks like the Hatracks don't care if they *are* spotted."

"No danger of that," Harrumph started complacently.

A sudden scrape of feet sounded behind them. Retief turned in time to see Lou leap up and dive for the fire control panel.

"We've been sold out!" he roared. "We're surrounded—!" Retief's jump knocked the big-nosed man spinning across the cabin—but not before he had swept his hand across half a dozen of the levers marked MISSLE-LAUNCH. Retief slammed the CANCEL switch, whirled to the screen to see swirling gases whipping from the sterns of six projectiles already lancing out at point-blank range for the targets racing alongside. Harrumph uttered a strangled hoot as the first struck home, detonated in a blinding eruption of raw energy. In quick succession, four more flashes whitened the screens—and a moment later the sixth. A thousand-cubic-mile volume of space was suddenly a boiling holocaust of white-hot debris and expanding gases.

"That did it," Jack yelped, and grabbed for a handhold as Retief sent the alien craft into a spine-wrenching turn hard aport.

"Hang on, everybody," he said between gritted teeth as the G forces mounted; the ship bucked, slewed into a wallow, righted itself—and gave a frantic lurch as a mighty hammer blow struck her, sent her into a vicious tumble.

"We're hit astern," Retief called. "Harrumph, how much of this can she take?"

"All iss losst!" the Haterakan gargled. "Ssuicidess! Murderss!"

The enemy fleet was dwindling on the screens now, the orderly formation scrambled into wild confusion by the sudden surprise onslaught. A Haterakan voice was croaking frantically from the comm unit. Harrumph scrambled to it, snorted and roared out a reply.

"I told Admiral it was all unfortunate error," he reported. "I explained that underling inadvertently depressed wrong key while attempting to tune telly. I don't think he believed me, alass!"

"We've got to get out," Lou shouted. "To the lifeboats!"

"He's right, Bully!" Jack seconded. "This thing'll break up any second now!"

"Impossible," Harrumph croaked. "Only two one-man life capssuless remain!"

"*I'm* getting out!" Lou lunged for a handhold, made it to the door.

"We can't leave Bully here by hisself!" Jack protested.

"Do as he says," Retief ordered. "Try to make it to Blue Moon and tip them to the Haterak strategy!"

"But—what about you, Bully?"

"I'll ride her down," Retief said. "Better get going now. Jawbone's counting on you!"

Lou and Jack pulled themselves through the door and were gone. Harrumph, making no move to follow, watched silently as Retief coaxed the immense tonnage of madly tumbling metal into a calmer spin, steadying the stricken vessel into a semblance of stability. The single still-functioning screen showed no pursuit from the disrupted armada.

"I've got about twenty percent control," Retief reported. "Harrumph, now's your chance to save that precious neck of yours. We'll try for Emporium. Take over the power panel and see what you can give me for atmospheric maneuvers!"

"It iss hopless—and yet—did I not mysself sselect you as prime survivor sspecimen?" The alien groped his way to his assigned station, swept the dials with an all-encompassing glance, his noodle-like fingers caressing the complex array of knobs and levers.

"Sstrange, you Terriess," he croaked. "It sseemss when death iss nearest, you fight mosst dessperately. Thiss iss hardly as advertised—and yet on thiss anomaly my life now dependss!"

4

An hour later the world ahead had swelled to a shimmering orb that filled the screens. New buffetings began, accompanied by a thin shriek of stratospheric gases. There was a rending sound as a mass of wreckage tore free, fell alongside the ship, glowing pink, then yellow, then flashing into metallic vapor.

"Power!" Retief called. "Everything you've got!"

"Alass, my poor enginess have taken their deathblow," Harrumph groaned. "But they yield up yet tiny trickle of mighty torrent that once they knew." The ship shook itself, fighting to swing into a tangential trajectory as she plunged deeper into the atmosphere. The shrilling of the thickening air became a bellow; far below, the surface of the planet rushed upward with frightful speed. A high cloud layer whipped past. Now the ship was hurtling on a long slant, stern foremost. Retief fed her power in short bursts, braking the falling derelict's velocity, forcing her into a flatter and flatter curve.

"That's all water down there," he called to Harrumph.

"Chartss sshow nearesst land mass liess four hundred miless disstant," Harumph trumpeted. "Too far!"

Now the ship was in an aerodynamic glide on her tiny emergency vanes, traveling at 1600 miles per hour at an altitude of 120,000 feet. Far ahead the horizon was an arch of blue against the black of space. The ship flashed on, into the darkness of the planet's night side; and still only the limitless dark sea lay below. On the panel, a faint glow indicated a distant planetary navigation beacon.

"Down to fifty thousand," Retief said. "We're good for maybe another couple of hundred miles."

"Insufficient," Harrumph grunted, watching the instruments.

The ship slowed, losing altitude rapidly now. Far ahead, ghostly whitecaps paced the ship, fell astern.

"We'll be about a mile short," Retief said calmly. "Harrumph, better go aft and get ready to jump."

"Sshall Fleetmaster of Haterak abandon hiss sship while mere Terry sstands by her?" the alien hooted. "No, smalleyed one; I sshare your folly!"

"In that case, give me one more boost astern and I'll admit you're a Powerman."

"I sshall try . . ." A moment later a faint surge lifted the dying vessel, palmed it forward; then, with a sharp explosion, all power died.

"Lock in!" Retief called, and threw the lever which dropped an ill-fitting shock frame over his chair. There was a long moment of suspense; then a violent impact, and the ship was slamming and shaking as she skimmed the wave tops. With a final shuddering plunge, the deck wallowed sideways, came to a stop with a crunching thud.

"We're aground." Retief flipped the hatch release; a surge of water boiled along the corridor, splashed into the command deck. Harrumph scrambled up, pulled himself through the opening. Retief followed, scaled the short ladder, emerged onto the sharply curved hull plates of the vessel's prow just as a wash of foam sluiced across it. He caught a glimpse of Harrumph's tall, ungainly figure scrambling for footing in the darkness; then the alien disappeared over the side with a choked yelp. Racing water ripped at Retief's legs; he gripped the hatch coaming, feeling a deep trembling through the hull underfoot. An ominous pounding swelled, became a muffled roar. From the darkness, a twenty-foot cliff of white water advanced, its curling top translucent in the starlight, driving a churning maelstrom ahead of it. The stranded ship stirred, slowly began a roll toward the oncoming wave, sucked by the incalculable forces of the vast tonnage of water. Retief balanced himself, watching the advancing comber; at the last possible instant, he took three running steps and dived into the high, glassy curve of the wave front as it swept over the spot where he had stood a moment before.

5

Retief drove forward, feeling himself rising with express train speed, up . . . up . . . He angled sharply down, gained a few yards of precious depth and was abruptly tumbling, whirling over and over, twisted and tossed like a chip in a millrace, caught in the turbulence of the breaking wave. He drew up his legs, wrapped his arms around them, and locked himself into a compact ball as the contending currents fought to rip him apart. Then, in a sudden instant of relative calm, he kicked out, lunged upward against the pressure of the water—and broke through into choppy white foam just below the pounding wave crest. He twisted, threw himself shoreward, arms outstretched and pointed, head down, body straight. Under his chest, the mighty engine of the comber churned with the power of a Niagara— but safely on top, Retief rode the breaker like a surfboard, throwing up a sparkling bow wave as he knifed through the water with the speed of a racing porpoise.

He raised his head for air, shook the water from his eyes; far ahead a great bonfire flared ruddily on the half-mile-distant beach. He twisted his body to aim toward it, shot at an angle across the face of the wave, almost enclosed in the whirling tube of water that arched over him.

The power of the wave diminished as it moved across the shelving sandbar, still driving Retief along as lightly as a straw. As it collapsed in a smother of bubbling foam, Retief found bottom, braced himself against the hip-deep waters now draining back, began the long wade in through the shallows toward the beach.

There was sudden flurry of movement to his left. He turned to see a flash of light reflected on a scaly, sinuous hide, a barrel-sized head with a tapered snout that ended in a circular mouth ringed with backward curving fangs.

As the creature's head rose, Retief leaped sideways, then threw himself at the predator as it struck, wrapping his arms around its foot-thick neck. At once, it writhed upward, lifting Retief clear of the water, then slammed back with a force that almost broke his grip. He held on, reached for a hold in the feathery gills he had seen just below the eyes.

The beast went mad, lashing the water in a wild contortion of whipping, twisting desperation. Retief crushed harder. The serpent attempted to dive, struck bottom, surfaced, swam madly in a circle. As it lifted its head to emit a harsh whistle, Retief shifted his grip, locked an arm under the jaw and levered up, with an effort that split the sodden jacket across his back. Cartilage creaked, snapped. The long body lashed once, violently, and was still.

As Retief rose, breathing hard, his mouth filled with the taste of bitter salt water, a beam of white light stabbed out from fifty feet distant, illuminating a thirty-foot circle of foam-flecked sea.

The next instant, with a sharp *carracckkk!* a shot ripped into the water inches from his body.

6

"Don't shoot him—yet!" a flat voice snapped. "Not unless he tries to get away."

Retief stood as still as the surging waters allowed, while a knife-prowed whaleboat swung in a wide curve to approach him, the light holding steady on him.

"All right—over the side, you!" the flat voice ordered. Hands reached to pull Retief into the boat. He looked around at a circle of tense faces which stared back in silence, looking him over.

"Grundy, latch onto that surf snake," a man with a mouth like a sliced muffin said over his shoulder. Men jumped to follow the order. The man who had spoken tucked the gun in the waistband of what looked like an expensive business suit, now sadly muddied and rumpled.

"Who are you, mister?" he barked. "Who sent you here? What were you after?"

"Do you gentlemen know anything about a tribe of E.T.'s known as the Haterak?" Retief inquired, wiping chilly salt water from his brow.

"What about 'em?" his captor asked sharply.

"There are ninety-four attack boats full of them cruising off Emporium at the moment," Retief said. "Their intentions aren't friendly to Terrans."

"Oh?" the man said noncommittally. "And where would you fit into the picture?"

"They shot me down. I made for your beacon."

The thin-lipped man looked at him, narrow-eyed.

"It seemed like a good idea at the time. I didn't have a lot of choice."

"Hey, Tully," the man called Grundy called from the stern of the boat. "I can't find a wound on this snake!"

"Looks to me like his neck's busted," another man contributed.

"First time I ever seen that," Grundy said wonderingly. "Must have dived and broken his neck on the bottom."

Tully held out his hand. "Let's have it," he grated. "The weapon you used on him."

Retief shook his head. "I can't help you there."

Tully's mouth tightened. "Grundy may believe in surf snakes

41

that commit suicide by pounding their heads against the bottom," he snapped. "I don't!" He jerked his head at a man standing by a worried-looking storekeeper-type with wide, round shoulders and chapped hands. "Russ, shake him down!"

Russ started to move toward Retief, glanced into his face, paused.

"Uh, look here, Tully, maybe we'd better wait until we're ashore to start any, uh, rough stuff."

"What rough stuff? I've got a gun on him!"

"Yeah, but—"

"I suggest we defer the crisis until later," Retief said. "I need to have a word with your planetary military authorities—"

"Never mind what you need," Tully barked. "All right, we'll get him ashore and deal with him there."

"I believe there's a CDT Mission here on Emporium," Retief said. "If you're shy about putting me in touch with your military men, just put a call through to the Consulate "

"Don't tell me what to do!" Tully snarled. "I know how to deal with your kind."

A moment later the boat's keel rasped against sand; the engines died to a soft mutter. Tully motioned Retief over the side. Surrounded by his captors, he waded up onto a sloping beach of coarse red sand.

Tully halted him by the bonfire where other men waited. Farther back, on a dune above the beach, a small space boat was parked, the legend EMPORIUM RESERVE PATROL lettered on its side, distinct in the glare of its ground lights.

"All right, you," Tully ordered. "Start talking."

"What about, Mr. Tully?" Retief said.

"I want to know who you're working for," the thin-lipped man rapped out. "Why you were sent here, how much that is, what you think you're going to find."

"What should I find, Mr. Tully?"

"Talk, damn you!"

"Sorry I can't oblige you," Retief said.

The gun jumped forward. "You'll talk, if I have to burn you into barbecue meat!"

"Nope," Retief said. "And after I'm barbecued, I'll be even more reticent."

"It's no use, Grundy said. "Ten to one he's working for "

"Shut up, damn you!"

"He couldn't talk if he wanted to, Grundy means," another man spoke up. "He'd be deep-hypnoed against it. I understand they have experts back at—"

"That's enough!" Tully yelled. "You bloody fools will tell him more than he'd find out in ten years!" He glared around at the others.

"Hey, Tully." A man carrying a field phone pushed through the crowd. "Here's Lonny reporting in . . ."

On the small screen of the portable rig a man's face appeared, his hair wet and dripping.

"We found it," he said excitedly. "Take a look!"

The hand-held camera angle shifted, showing an expanse of dark sea with whitecaps; then it submerged to follow the glimmering of an underwater searchlight as it played over a dark shape looming among waving sea fronds on the bottom.

"Here she is," the narrator said, his voice muffled now by his breathing mask. "You can see for yourself. It's a Hatrack assault boat!"

Tully's eyes narrowed.

"Just where do you stand?" he inquired rhetorically. He turned to a moon-face man.

"Horner, make a call to . . . you know where, and see what they say."

Horner nodded and went across to a parked ground car. Five minutes passed in tense silence before he started back.

"We're to hold him for the police," he called. "They'll be along directly."

It was less than ten minutes before the sound of an approaching engine was audible. A tracked vehicle pulled up beside the bonfire in a cloud of dust. Half a dozen men in dark uniforms bearing Planetary Police badges descended, guns prominently displayed. The NCO in charge, a squat man with gaps between his teeth, looked Retief over with a grin.

"O.K., we'll take care of this pigeon, Tully," he said in a thick voice.

"Sergeant Roscoe, you *are* going to take him back to headquarters for questioning?" Tully asked anxiously. He seemed half afraid of the armed men. "I think it's important we discover just what his coming here means . . ."

"Hell, no!" the squat man spat between his teeth, hitched up his gun belt. "Not that it's any of your business—my orders are to take him back in the dunes and shoot him!"

7

The NCO briskly told off a firing-squad detail, formed them up in a square with Retief, handcuffed, at the center, and marched them off along the beach. Half a mile from the bonfire he halted them.

"This spot suit you O.K., pal?" he inquired of Retief with a grin. He jerked a thumb at a line of sand hills nearby. "Those dunes'll stop the slugs; and it'll be easy digging, afterwards."

"An admirable choice," Retief said pleasantly. "Better check the other side first, just in case there's a party of young ladies changing their clothing for a moonlight swim."

"Nood dames, huh?" Roscoe grinned mirthlessly, sauntered closer to Retief, poked the muzzle of the automatic weapon into the diplomat's side. "You wouldn't rib me, would you, buddy?"

"I just wanted to say a word to you privately," Retief said softly. "It's about money."

Roscoe licked thick lips. "What you got in mind?"

"You seem like a trustworthy soul; I have a sizable amount of cash in a safe-deposit box, under another name; I'd like to see that it gets to my Aunt Prunie. If you'd just take my key along, you can collect it and pass it on to good old Auntie. Try my left hip pocket; I can't quite reach it; the handcuffs, you know..."

"Yeah, they're kind of confining, pal. Left hip pocket, that was?" Roscoe reached—and Retief brought an elbow up in a sharp blow to the solar plexus. As the man *oof!*ed and leaned against him, Retief twisted far enough to grab the gun awkwardly with his manacled hands, rammed it into the man's chest.

"Hold it right there, fellows," he said as the other men jumped toward him. "If I were you, Roscoe," he added, "I wouldn't wiggle one teentsy little muscle."

"You're nuts," one of the men said hoarsely. "This won't buy you nothing. We got five guns on you."

"Better toss them in a neat little pile," Retief said. "Otherwise your colleague gets a new aperture to breathe through."

"Don't do what he says," one of the men, wearing corporal's stripes, snapped. "He's bluffing!"

"Yeah, Lum—but if he ain't...," another demurred.

"Roscoe wouldn't want it no other way," Lum stated flatly. "Right, Roscoe?"

The addressee made a gobbling noise.

"Roscoe, drop the key to the cuffs in my pocket," Retief ordered.The sergeant complied.

"All right, fan out," Lum was ordering the men. "Goldie, you take the left; Satch, you take the right. When I give the word—"

A brilliant flash lit up the sky behind the men. A moment later, a sharp shock jarred the ground underfoot. Then a long, crashing *baroom!* echoed across the sands.

"Cheeze! Sabotage!" The four cops started toward the sound.

"As you were, you bone-skulls!" Lum roared. "We—" Something came flying through the air. past Retief and smacked against the corporal's head with a dull thud. He staggered and went to all fours.

"Ssssst! Thiss way, Bully West!" a hoarse voice hissed from the darkness. The four policemen had halted, were gaping uncertainly at their fallen comrade. Retief pushed Roscoe away, cracked the barrel of the machine pistol across the side of the man's head as he made a grab for the weapon, then turned and sprinted for the shelter of the dunes, while four guns racketed belatedly behind him.

4

"Over here!" The tall, thin-legged figure of Harrumph loomed up among the sand heaps, his sodden tunic hanging open, the loops of braid at wrist and neck hanging awry, his boots scuffed, his cap missing.

Retief dived for cover as a wild shot sent a shower of molten sand flying from the dune crest above him.

"I see you're a swimmer after all," he said. "What was the big boom back there?"

"We Hateraks are equally at home on land, under sea, and in space," the alien croaked. "As for diverssion, I made ssmall adjusstment to power regulator of ground car. Follow me; there iss ssand-crab burrow just here..." He turned and moved off, upended abruptly, and disappeared. Retief followed as more shots lit the dunes in flashes; he saw a dark opening ahead, pushed his way into a narrow passage that slanted sharply down. Ahead, a dim light gleamed and flickered.

"It'ss trifle cramped," Harrumph's voice echoed softly, "but passable."

For the next ten minutes, Retief wormed his way through a maze of twisting, turning, dipping tunnels, following the Haterakan's lead. They emerged onto a wind-swept stretch of rocky sand above the deserted beach, half a mile from the light of the bonfire. Far away, faint shouts and probing hand-lights marked the position of the thwarted firing squad.

"Thanks," Retief said. "You happened by at a convenient moment."

"I followed you," Harrumph corrected. "After all, you ssaved me from wrath of ssavage Lou—and you're only Terry to whom I dare sshow my face." He waggled his head. "I musst confess, I find your folkwayss insscrutable."

"There are times when I find them less than scrutable myself," Retief conceded.

Harrumph wagged his outlandish head sadly. "I embarked on thiss mad adventure in misstaken belief it wass jolly game, offering abundance of loot at minimum risk. Now I find actual bulletss sshot at me, in persson! Ssuch dissillusionment!"

"You're lucky our Mr. Magnan isn't here," Retief said sympathetically. "He plans to throw everything in the book at you."

"Disstressing newss! It iss plain that I musst ssomehow contact Grand Admiral and pass along thiss information!" The Fleetmaster clacked his shredders together. "Hmm. I have proposssal: for the nonce, inasmuch as we are both hunted fugitivess, let uss join forcess, proceed to Haterak, and deliver newss to Grand Admiral before it iss too late!"

"I suppose it might save some bloodshed," Retief said. "In a way it is a little unsportsmanlike to tempt an inoffensive galaxy-conqueror into folly."

"I musst warn you," Harrumph said sternly. "Make no attempt to ssway me from path of duty, jusst because you Terries like to fight!"

"I wouldn't think of interfering," Retief said. "After all, you did bean Roscoe with a coconut on my behalf."

"True. Very well, then: it'ss ssettled: we're alliess until further notice—provided we can find way to depart these hostile sshoress."

Retief looked toward the encampment across the sands. "I think we'll have to rely on Mr. Tully to supply our transportaion, he said. " Come on, Harrumph; let's find out what kind of guard he mounts."

2

From a distance of fifty yards, Retief surveyed the bright-lit stretch of turf where the small ERP vessel was parked, bathed in the harsh glare of its polyarcs. Two armed men patrolled at opposite sides of the area.

"How fast can you run?" Retief inquired in a whisper of his companion.

"Not very, I fear. At last physsical tessting, I turned in misserable performance; almosst ten ssecondss for hundred-yard dassh."

"Good enough," Retief encouraged. "Suppose you go to the far side of the pad and create a small diversion; then make it back as fast as you can. I'll try to have the door open."

"And if not?"

"Then just keep going."

"Very well; I'll do my besst . . . " The alien slipped away in the darkness.

Retief lay low; the nearer guard paced past, craning his neck back across the field toward the spot where smoke was still rising from the smoldering car. He halted suddenly, brought his gun up as a faint cry rang from the dunes a hundred yards away. At a second cry, he set off at a run, as did the other sentry. At once, Retief came to his feet, sprinted to the launch's entry lock, exposed in the full glare of the lights. The outer door, a standard Gendye Mark XI installation, was firmly locked.

From one of the pouches clipped to the belt of his shipsuit, Retief took a small steel tape; quickly, he scaled dimensions on the panel, located a point, marked it with a fine-pointed marker. From the dunes a shout rang out, followed by a shot.

Retief tucked the scale away, took out a minaturized laser cutter, focused the needle-fine beam at a precise angle on the metal. Under the sun-bright point of ruby light, the metal hissed into vapor. Now Retief could hear confused yelling, punctuated by a yelp of pain.

The hole bored, he took out a six-inch length of fine wire, inserted it in the aperture, delicately tickled the mechanism inside the massive door. There was a decisive *click!* and the panel swung outward. Retief swarmed up inside the boat as pounding feet approached along the turf. Harrumph rounded the stern of the vessel, all four legs working like pistons, with an incredible bound gained the open lock. Retief slammed the valve home behind him, dashed for the control compartment. He flipped switches, felt the deck of the small vessel quiver under him as the drive unit warmed. A red panel light warned HOLD.

"Hey! I read a telltale light on Number 28," a startled voice broke from the speaker above his head. "Who's that out there?"

"Just spot-checking you," Retief answered airily. "Glad to see you're on the ball in Control."

"Nobody never tells me nothing," the voice grumbled. A moment later the red warning light winked off and a green READY replaced it.

"Hey!" the speaker rasped. "I just checked the duty-roster, and it don't show no inspection crew working tonight! Who are you?"

"Sorry, I'm not at liberty to disclose that information," Retief said as he palmed the LAUNCH-FINAL lever home. "When you see Tully, just tell him his play-pretty has been commandeered by the Corps Diplomatique for offical use. I'm sure he'll understand." With a surge and a roar, the tiny boat lifted from the ramp and hurtled skyward at two and one half gees.

3

Haterak was a pale green planet swinging in a wide orbit around a vast blue star. Harrumph crouched over the screen as the ship hurtled in past the series of pock-marked moons the big world had captured in past millennia.

"Behold, Bully West!" he chortled. "It iss pleassant aspect, if I do ssay sso mysself!"

"Better key in your fleet IFF," Retief said. "After dodging Terran gunboats for the first half of the trip, it would be somewhat of an anticlimax to be downed by your Coast Guard now."

"Ahh, how ssurprissed Grand Admiral will be to see me ssafe and ssound. Poor fellow, how he must have grieved, believing me losst forever!"

"Having gotten you back, I hope he listens attentively to what you have to tell him," Retief said.

"But of course! My admiral and I are boon companions! Many time we've caroused night away together, uttering subtle witticisms and fingering oddly-shaped kiki stones, while soaking our toes in scented soda-water!"

"With a bond like that, you can't miss," Retief conceded.

Harrumph made the series of rubbery sounds which indicated mirth.

"As for you, Bully, I'm ssure your baroque ssense of humor will endear you to him. He'll ssecure memorable yock when I recount to him your parting word to that atrocious Tully creature!" The Haterakan emitted snorts and hisses expressing uncontrollable hilarity. "Commandeered by Corps Diplomatique, indeed!" he hooted. "Imagine simple, uncouth creature of violence such as yourself in role of diplomat! Hroomph, roomphfff, unnphffs, phsumphs! It iss priceless jape, Bully!" Abruptly the laughter ceased. The alien rolled a faceted eye reflectively at Retief.

"On other hand," he said, "why not? My people are not noted for their hosspitality to sub-Haterakans, I musst confess; but if I present you as official emmissary of Terranss my admiral will of coursse resspect protocols due alien envoy!"

"Well—if you really think I could carry it off . . ." Retief said.

"It'ss worth a try," Harrumph said. "Jusst look inscrutable and let me do talking."

He turned to the screen where a flock of fast-moving blips were coming up from the planet, flipped his mike key, grunted out a message in his native tongue. A sharp reply broke from the speaker.

"Ah, Admiral iss planning ssomething little sspecial for me," the alien said in a pleased tone. "He directss me to rendezvous with escort at ten thousand miless out. Probably he planss to award me new decoration for unussual sservicess to the Archarch! Knee-clasp with pendant to bubble of Order of Ip-ip-hashoo perhaps!"

"A heart-warming prospect, I'm sure," Retief commented.

They watched the screens as the swarming vessels rose to meet them, formed up to englobe the launch. There were more exchanges via phone. Harrumph made a contented buzzing noise, rasping his vestigial wings together.

"It sseems Admiral iss going all-out to do me honor," he confided to Retief. "We have esscort fit for Archarch himsself!"

Flanked by the dark finger shapes of the Haterakans, the boat arrowed down into a soupy atmosphere, broke through thick cloud cover over a glassy violet sea. Following instructions relayed by Harrumph, Retief guided the vessel across a rocky coast, passed low over the jagged crests of a mountain range.

"Ssignal honor!" Harrumph cackled. "We're to be permitted to bypass port area and land within fortress itsself, mosst clossely guarded ultimate ssecurity area on planet! Thiss iss even more gratifying tribute than I expected!"

Retief steered the boat across desiccated mud flats, closely followed by the escorting vessels, settled in a cloud of dust within a circle of massive, towering walls.

"Now, jusst watch me," Harrumph said, "and when camerass pan your way, wiggle your earss. It will be interpreted as reassuring gessture of humility." He studied Retief's features. "It would help if you could extrude your eyeballss, as well, but I ssuppose you'd find that awkward."

"How would it be if I just extruded my tongue instead?"

"Proposal doess you credit, Bully—but I don't wish you to appear *too* sservile. After all, you *are* Terran Ambassador." He twitched his shredding hooks in the Haterakan equivalent of a wink.

As they stepped down from the boat onto hard-baked clay, a rank of gaudily painted aliens in elaborate gold helmets ornamented with silver quills advanced, holding compact power guns tipped with double-pronged, barbed bayonets at the ready.

"Impressive dissplay, eh," Harrumph clucked. "I suppose we'd besst wait for Admiral to appear before reviewing Honor Guard." Harrumph gazed placidly at the troops as they halted with a clatter of accouterments, their swordtipped weapons bare inches from the alien's ribby chest.

"These fellows are trifle overzealous," he muttered to Retief. "Quality of consscriptss one sees these dayss iss sscandalouss!"

A tall Haterakan stalked into view, spectacularly decked out in a fantastic display of silver greaves and plumes and spikes and ribbons, his spurred feet clacking as he walked. At sight of the impressive figure, Harrumph emitted a pleased buzz.

"Ah! Here is Grand Admiral Hikop himsself! Ssplendid chap, Bully! I know you and he will become besst of chumss, if only we can resstrain him from hacking you to pieces on ssight!"

The Admiral advanced, flanked by a quartet of gaudily

bedecked aides. Ten feet from Retief and Harrumph he halted, pointed with outstretched claw, and emitted a rumble like a dormant volcano stirring to life. At once, the ring of bayonets leaped forward, hemming in Retief and his Haterakan guide with a bristling ring of needle-points. Harrumph uttered an astonished bleat.

"A dramatic ceremony," Retief said admiringly. "When do you get the medal?"

"Ssomething...ssomething is amiss!" the alien croaked. "Admiral musst have been jessting!"

"What did he say?"

"Unless my ssenssess deceived me," Harrumph choked, "he said, 'Truss that traitorouss ssaboteur in chainss—and enemy sspy with him!'"

5

In the olive-hued gloom of the tall, narrow Inquisition Chamber, seven Haterakan judges stared down at the accused from their high perches, their oversized yellow eyes shining with an eerie fluorescence.

"Thiss iss fantasstic!" Harrumph croaked. "That Masster of Fleet ssuch as mysself sshould be ssubjected to ssuch indiginities, jusst becausse sship I was nominally captaining at time happened to launch few unscheduled torpedoess! If thosse sskin-headss commanding had been more alert, they wouldn't have been blassted out of sspace!" The Haterakan shifted position, causing his chains to clank dismally. He groaned, a sound like mud gurgling down a drain. "And I assured you of ssafe conduct, Bully! Insstead, you, too, will sshortly dangle from VIP torture racks besside me!" He made a harsh buzzing sound, indicating heartfelt emotion. "They go too far, when thuss they ssully honor of member of noble Avunculate of Meticulously Husbanded Wisdom!"

"Don't feel too badly," Retief said comfortingly. "This won't be the first diplomatic mission that ended up hanging on somebody's wall."

"Glorrff! When I contemplate vines of ambition withering, neglected, in my Garden of Future Achievements, never now to be brought to blossom—!" Harrumph clashed his chains despairingly. "Thuss are mighty fallen, Bully West. And all because that ssoft-witted, near-sighted, ssanctimoniouss incompetent who calls himsself Grand Admiral of Conquering Horde woke up on wrong side of the hibernating rack!" He ceased his laments as the doors swung wide, admitting the tall orange, gold, and purple enameled figure of the Admiral. As he passed Harrumph, the latter emitted a sharp hissing sound and rattled out a little tune on his claw, then delivered a cacophonous speech. The Admiral clicked his shredders in an unmistakably contemptuous gesture and snorted a reply, then clambered to his waiting perch.

"I told him," Harrumph relayed, "that a sslight misscalculation hass occurred, and advissed him that he hass Terran Ministser Plenipotentiary in ironss; but I fear he was unimpressed."

There was another guttural exchange.

"The Admiral hass taken leave of his ssensess!" Harrumph translated. "He states that it iss pointless to bother about protocol now, ssince in very near future all Terrans will be sslaves of Haterak! I've explained hiss misstake to him, but he sspurnss my warning!"

"Please express to the Admiral my hope that he'll bring along something more impressive than the peashooters I've seen so far," Retief directed. "I'm afraid they wouldn't even give our immense fleets of late-model planet-busters a warm-up."

"He ssayss," Harrumph relayed after the exchange, "that your ssufferingss musst have desstroyed your witss; it iss well known that Terries are afflicted with massive neurossiss which compellss them to disstribute fruits of their effortss to any who dessire sshare in loot, firsst come, firsst sserved. He intendss not to be ssecond."

"Kindly advise His Excellency that I'm delighted at the prospect of his providing us with some useful target practice. But caution him not to try to sneak away at the last moment to avoid battle. That sort of thing sends our ferocious fighters into a frenzy."

The Admiral barked a furious reply when the warning had been delivered.

"All iss losst!" Harrumph groaned. "In hiss arrogance, he boasstss that the combined Imperial Fleets now massing off Blue Moon will sseize planet in twenty-five hourss from now, after which they will proceed in victoriouss ssweep to annex remainder of Terran-occupied worldss in clusster!"

"An amusing conceit," Retief commented. "Ask him what kind of firepower he imagines will suffice to overcome our massed armadas of invincible world-wreckers."

In heartbroken tones, Harrumph relayed the Admiral's triumphant summary of his armaments: "Poor deluded ssimpleton hass at hiss command sseventy-ssix firsst- line battle cruissers, one hundred and eighteen class W destroyers, and a hosst of lesser vessels, all fully manned and ready to sset ssail— not that he'll required more than fraction of his force to reduce one misserable planet."

"Tell him I admire his spirit," Retief said. "It's not much fun administering a drubbing to whiners."

One of the judges clacked his shredders in an impatient way and snuffled out a curt suggestion.

"Hé says, 'Enough of this balderdash!'" Harrumph translated. "'Let trial begin!'"

At once, the Grand Admiral spoke up, pointing first at Harrumph and then at Retief.

"He says that I ssold out to imperialistss, in person of you, Bully," Harrumph relayed. "And that you in turn are guilty of subversion, espionage, and being Terran."

The judges looked at each other, nodded, then rose and began filing from the chamber with the air of persons who have completed a bothersome chore.

"Rather early in the trial for a coffee break, isn't it?" Retief inquired.

"Trial is over," Harrumph corrected gloomily.

"What was the verdict?"

"Guilty, of course. You don't think judges would want to annoy Grand Admiral by arguing with him?"

"You people are to be congratulated on your legal system," Retief said admiringly. "Under similar circumstances, we Terries would have taken three weeks of hearing evidence to reach the same conclusion. By the way, what's the sentence?"

"What else?" Harrumph said gloomily. "Death! By torture!"

2

The VIP torture suite was an underground installation, hung with life-size photographs of bedraggled former victims. Admiral Hikop, accompanied by two assistants in ominous black leathers, entered the room as the armed guards completed the task of attaching the prisoners' manacles to hooks set overhead in the damp plastic walls. He mounted a perch of polished metal rods, leaned back at ease, and spoke offhandedly to Harrumph.

"He ssayss," the latter announced in tones of imminent doom, "that we sshall now ssee who whinerss are. Prepare yoursself, Bully; now tormentss begin!"

The two technicians had busily set about erecting a small apparatus resembling a primitive phonograph. Carefully, they aimed its bell-shaped horn at the two manacled victims.

"Ssummon all you ressolve now," Harrumph said. "Thiss iss going to ssmart!"

"What's he going to do, play old Ethel Merman records?"

"It'ss droonge projector," the Haterakan croaked. "One of our mosst ssophissticated information-extracting devicess..." He broke off as a pale light sprang up from the projector, accompanied by a soft humming sound. Retief felt a faint tingle of the scalp, as though someone had raked fingernails across a dry blackboard. Beside him, Harrumph quivered and clashed his shredders together.

"My veeperss—will be garbled...for life..." he gasped out, "How sstoically you endure agony, Bully!"

"The reputation of humanity is at stake," Retief pointed out. "It wouldn't do to reveal what I'm going through right now."

"Of coursse not; and your example sstiffenss my ressolve!" Harrumph drew himself up, only a slight twitiching of his oversized oculars reflecting his sufferings.

"One day I will even sscore with treacherouss Hikop!" he hissed. "Not content with betraying me into embarrassing position of looking up small end of my own ceremonial ssmall-arm, wretch now sseekss to sstrip me—number two man in Haterakan fleet—of lasst sshredss of dignity! But let him do his worsst—I will ssurvive—and one day sseek him out and extract vengeance in full!"

Abruptly, the Admiral snapped a command and the droonge projector clicked off.

"Moral victory, Bully," Harrumph called hoarsely. "But brace yoursself; next one will be worsse!"

Now the technicians wheeled the projector aside, drew a device resembling a xylophone into position.

"No, not that!" Harrumph hissed. "The Ordeal of Forty-one Sstenchess! Ultimate in olfactory atrocitiess! He wouldn't! Not to old kiki-sstone fingering buddy!"

"He's lost all sense of proportion," Retief commiserated. "But let's not give him the satisfaction of seeing us cry."

"If mere Terry can face his fate thuss, can I do less?" the alien inquired rhetorically, straightening his back. The Admiral's aides were busily adjusting plastic pads over their lateral orifices to protect themselves from the effluvia about to be released. The torturer tilted up the first tube in the rack—a livid blue cylinder an inch in diameter and eight inches long—and with a flourish twisted the nozzle. A heavy bluish vapor jetted toward the captives. Retief sniffed, caught a faint odor of wet wool.

"Gornch-lizard musk," Harrumph gasped. "Ghasstly!"

The next tube, bright green, emitted a chartreuse mist with a scent not unlike that of kosher salami.

"That reminds me," Retief said. "We haven't had lunch."

"Such verve," the Haterakan croaked. "To assay jape while engulfed in unattenuated reek of Gluglu plant!"

In quick succession then, the technicians uncapped red, pink, violet, orange tubes, exposing the torturees to essences resembling overheated tires, burnt toast, chow mein, and aged Gorgonzola.

"Hold on . . . jusst little longer," Harrumph wheezed. "Ssoon our ssenssibilitiess will be deadened by very violence of on-slaught!"

"I'm hoping against hope he doesn't give us a shot of attar of government office," Retief said.

The Admiral and his helpers conferred in guttural tones as the exhaust fans whirled the last of the flavors away; then the workers aimed an immense yellow tube, reached gingerly to uncap it, and jumped back. An ocher emanation boiled forth, whipped into Retief's face, bringing a choking, dry-as-dust smell of cobwebs and musty bindings. Harrumph gave a despairing cry and writhed in his chains. The Admiral uttered a clatter of harsh laughter.

"One day villain will pay for thiss," Retief's fellow sufferer gasped out. "Bully, do you still live?"

"Just barely," Retief said. "That last one almost did the job. Unless I'm mistaken, it was the authentic odor of sanctity."

"He'ss done hiss worsst now," Harrumph said weakly. "Future can hold no terrorss, sstink-wise."

"It looks as though he's shifting his attack," Retief pointed out, as the busy torturers removed the racked tubes and replaced them with a sturdy easel. One lifted a covered retangle into place, then carefully averted his oversized eyes and whipped off the cover to reveal a garish composition of pink and yellow lozenges.

"I might have known," Harrumph said in a tortured tone. "Now we face trial of Abominable Pigmentations! At thiss moment I envy you your retractable eyeskinss, Bully. As for me— I musst ssteel mysself to endure unprotected impact of visual nightmares on my naked ocularss!"

"We're in this together," Retief said. "I'll demonstate Terran endurance by staring fearlessly at whatever he throws at us."

"Nobly sspoken, Bully! But I warn you Admiral Hikop, once aroussed, is merciless!" He watched in fascinated horror as the first visual torture was removed and a second took its place, this one a pattern of sour green and muddy orange.

"Thiss vile concatenation of chartreuse, tangerine, gorfal, bleem, and tizrall iss product of a dissordered mind!" Harrumph choked. "I'm not ssure I can sstand up to pace, Bully! If I collapse and begin babbling, try to find it in your circulatory pump to forgive me!"

"I wouldn't blame you, Harrumph," Retief reassured the distressed alien. "At the last exhibit of neo-pop art sponsored by our CulturalAttaché, strong men broke down and cried, and some of the pieces weren't much worse than this."

For a nerve-wrenching quarter of an hour, the ocular bombardment continued, while Harrumph whimpered and groaned piteously. At last, after a peculiarly hideous presentation featuring Mexican pink and jade green spirals, the ordeal ended. The easel was set aside, and an ominously massive apparatus erected in its stead. A technician flipped switches, and a deep growling noise started up, slowly ascended the scale to a shrill screech, then faded to inaudibility. Harrumph quivered, his chains rattling like castanets. His eyes jerked, rolled up and set; he slumped in his fetters. Only then did the machine wail back down to a groan that trailed off into silence.

"Forgive me," Harrumph gasped weakly, struggling to an upright position. "I've always been . . . peculiarly sensitive . . . to snarf-vibrations."

"They were rough, all right," Retief agreed. "I'd have dropped too, if I hadn't been toughened up by years of violin cadenzas and ambassadorial pep talks."

The Admiral spoke harshly to his men now, pointing at Retief. The specialists attempted to snort replies, but the obviously incensed official shouted them down.

"Alass, Bully," Harrumph interpreted the byplay. "If your intention wass to impress the Admiral with your sstubborness, you ssucceeded all to well. Your contempt for physical ssuffering, he ssays, iss implied reproach to all Haterakanss. He therefore decreess that you—and I as well, as your associate in crime—are to be casst into Arena of the Ravenous Predators, there to be torn, living, limb from limb!"

3

It was gray dawn when the armored truck in which Retief and his companion in misfortune were confined rumbled through the high gates of the arena. Through the bars, Retief looked up at the towering oval of gray concrete, set with steep tiers of perches, row on row, that mounted upward toward the foggy sky. Except for the plumbers' nightmare of rods in place of benches, it looked much as such theaters had always looked, from the Colosseum at Rome to the Grand Corrida at Northroyal.

"We'll be working to good housse, if that'ss any conssolation,"Harrumph croaked dolefully. "Entire Grand Paternalate will turn out to ssee broken Fleetmaster and alien spy meet their colorful dooms."

"What time does the first show go on?" Retief inquired.

"At noon, ssharp; about three hourss from now," the Haterakan said. "There won't be ssecond—not for uss."

"What will we be up against?"

"Traditionally, ceremoniess will open with dire-beast in good appetite. If either of uss sshould ssurvive meeting—unlikely eventuality—I imagine they'll bring on brace of bull-devils fitted with tempered chromalloy horn tips, and finish up with flock of meat-hawks, to dissposse of any leftoverss."

"Sounds like a well-balanced program. What will we have to defend ourselves with?"

"Wooden stavess. If we wissh to whittle pointss on them with our teeth, we're at liberty to do sso."

"What if we win?"

"In that case, the Admiral will be doubly annoyed. Sstill, sshort of ssupernatural intervention, the problem iss unlikely to arisse."

As the cart splashed across the pavement, where a half-inch film of water sparkled in place of sand, Retief studied the layout of the vast stadium, noting the steep ramps leading up to the topmost bleachers, the dark rectangles of doors at intervals along the base, the ominous barred openings situated directly beneath an elaborately decorated box.

"Harrumph, how much do you know about the design of the place?" he asked.

"Under circumstancess, your curiosity sseems ssomewhat morbid," the alien replied glumly. "Still, as it happenss, I wass one of ssupervissors assigned to oversssee consstruction of Recreation Center. Ah, how long ago it sseemss! I wass but youth, sscarce sshed of my gills, sstill moist with broth of forcing vatss..."

"A most emotional homecoming for you, I'm sure," Retief acknowledged. "But to get back to specifics..."

"Recreation Center is in heart of city," Harrumph said indifferently. "Conveniently located to afford facilities for wholesome pastimes to young and old at all hours of day and night. Arena occupies central position, surrounded by game rooms, sporting areas, eat-and-drinkeries, shops..." He waved a member at the bleachers. "Under stands are private club areas, dressing rooms, pro shops, and the like."

"What about guards?"

"They'll be possted at all exitss. Alsso, arena officals and event promoterss who contracted with Grand Admiral for our sservicess will occupy box, jusst there, accompanied by alert bodyguardss." He pointed. "And of course, Hikop himsself and hiss toadiess will be gloating down, well-armed, from jusst above gate."

"What's back of the gate?"

"Private passage for use of big sshotss. It leadss to club areas and on to limoussine entrance."

"What's behind those small doors over there?"

"Passagess leading to the sservice areass; they're used by the maintenance perssonel, mainly."

"They're not used during the show?"

"A few of them..." Harrumph proceeded to outline the procedures and practices followed in the conduct of a typical Games.

"We'll probably follow sslingsshot and garbage-can lid event," he concluded. "By that time fanss will be getting resstless, and ready for some real action, which you and I will provide by our pathetic effortss to esscape our inevitable endss."

"Buck up, Harrumph," Retief encouraged the other. "As you pointed out earlier, you're a representative of a proud Avunculate; you're not going to let the Admiral see you go to pieces."

"An unfortunate choise of wordss, in view of the dire-beast's habit of dismembering hiss victimss with ssingle sstroke of hiss dreadfull tusskss; but you're right." The alien's hoarse voice took on a firmer timbre. "Never let it be said that Fleetmaster Harrumph sshowed purple glimp-scale in hour of hiss trial!"

The tumbrel reached an archway, rolled into deep shadow. A detail of guards with guns alertly aimed herded the two prospective gladiators along a short, musty passage into a dark cell, clanged the door shut behind them, then took up their posts just outside.

"Dissmal sspot in which to spend our lasst hourss," Harrumph said dejectedly. "Sstill, we can hold our banners high for yet little while, Bully. I ssuggesst we pass time by ssinging ribald ssongss at top of our respiratory organss. It may not help our ssituation, but at leasst it will bug hell out of guardss."

4

For two hours, the crowd noises from beyond the barred door had been steadily increasing in volume. The guards had withdrawn half an hour earlier, immediately after which several parties of brilliantly painted notables had come along the dark passage to peer in at the prisoners and loudly discuss their probable performances.

"Big money gamblerss," Harrumph explained glumly. "Every extra ssecond we ssurvive against beasstss will earn one of thesse parassitess nice piece of change."

The objects of the bettors' interest watched as the wagerers exchanged colorful strips of high-denomination credit to back their predictions. One, in flashy orange and electric blue, called Retief in the Lesser Obfuscese, a widely used trade dialect.

"You there, fellow! I have a proposition for you. When the dire-beast makes his first charge, you step in and trip up this renegade crony of yours. While the carnivore is busy worrying his remains, you can enjoy a few extra seconds of joyous existence at his expense, while I'll net a pretty profit by backing the underdog. What say? How does the scheme strike you?"

"I've got a better idea," Retief said. "Slip us a couple of power guns and we'll confound the bookmakers by shooting up the menagerie, and bagging a few assorted customers as well."

"An interesting suggestion..." The sportsman clacked his shredders thoughtfully. "But too risky; I might possibly be held in some way responsible in the event you were caught with the weapons. Still..." He glanced around conspiratorily. "I'll give the matter some thought..."

"What wass that rasscal Rukktooey ssaying to you, Bully?" Harrumph demanded as the bookmaker moved on. "I caution you: he iss sscoundrel of firsst magnitude."

"We're just nattering about the odds. He seems to have an idea they might change suddenly."

"I supposse thesse ghouls loitering about our prisson have noted my exceptional physsical development," Harrumph mused. "I've good mind to upsset their calculationss by hurling mysself into jawss of firsst beasst to appear."

"Don't do anything hasty," Retief cautioned. "We're not beaten yet."

"Only few minutes now," Harrumph croaked nervously, pressing his horny skull against the bars to observe the patch of sunlight glaring at the end of the passage. "I'm not ssure whether I'm impatient to have it over with, or petrified at prosspect..." He recoiled abruptly, his eyes quivering with sudden panic.

"I've made up my mind," he said. "I'm petrified; they're coming!"

A moment later, there was a stealthy rasp of feet; the gaudy blue and orange color scheme of Rukktooey appeared. The speculator's manner was distinctly furtive.

"Quick!" he hissed. "I was unable to manage any firearms on such short notice, but I've got something better—and far less conspicuous." He fumbled under his rib-cape.

"Bully—don't trust rasscal!" Harrumph exclaimed—too late. Rukktooey had already whipped out a small pistol-shaped object, aimed the slim, silvery barrel at Retief and pressed the firing stud. There was a soft *tsssp!* of compressed gas and a jet of something cool, smelling of mint, sprayed in his face, stinging his eyes and nose.

"It's a potent drug—a neuronic sensitizer," the bookie hissed, looking over his narrow, sloping shoulder. "Quite illegal, of course, but much favored by groog players and other sleight-of-hand artists. Probably fatal in the end to Terries, of course, but in your case it hardly matters, eh?" As the gambler spoke, Retief felt a curious sensation sweep over him—as if the air in the room had suddenly thickened. The shadows deepened to a dusky, somehow luminous crimson gloom. The sound of the crowd had taken on a remote, wailing quality that sank to a lugubrious moan.

"...find...it...use...ful...innn...deeteectiiinnngggg..." The gambler's voice, sinking to a deep baritone, then a rumbling bass, wound down like a failing tape recorder to a thrumming which dwindled to a profound silence. The entrepreneur himself stood frozen in mid-motion, the gas gun half lowered, his vocalizing orifice gaping comically.

Retief turned to Harrumph—not without effort; his head seemed suddenly as unwieldy as a Halloween pumpkin. The Haterakan was poised eerily in mid-air, his feet clear of the floor, arrested in mid-leap toward the bookie. From somewhere, a deep subsonic beat seemed to reverberate ponderously through the floor and walls.

Retief turned his attention to Rukktooey. The Haterakan still posed just beyond the bars, as rigid as a clothes tree. Retief reached between the bars, lifted the gun carefully from his grasping member, examined it. It was not precisely heavy, but a massive inertia made it difficult to move. There was a screw cap at the base of the grip. Retief twisted hard at it, without apparent success. As he took his hand away, the cap stirred, slowly rotated free. Inside the hollow it had covered, three white pea-sized spheres were visible. Retief dug them out, sniffed, caught the faint mint odor. He forced them into his pocket, finding the cloth as stiff as sheet lead, while the gas pellets had a tendency to float unsupported in the air. He checked over the bookmaker's pockets, turning up a small container of irrregularly bent rods, clearly keys, which he pocketed. Then he replaced the gas gun in Rukktooey's hand and stood by, watching for signs of returning motion and gauging the passage of subjective time.

After what seemed about ten minutes, he noticed that the alien's gun hand was coming down slowly, then faster. At the same time, the low throb of background sound quickened to a rumble, became the mutter, then the roar of the impatient audience.

"...ccchhheeatiingg onn the part of their opponents." Rukktooey's voice rose to normal as he briskly tucked away the dart gun. Beside Retief, Harrumph, surging forward, made a grab between the bars, missed as the gambler drew back with a dry clicking of laughter.

"The *inth* will take effect in a few minutes," the latter said to Retief. "It produces a ten percent improvement in Harterakan perceptivity and reflexes. It will probably be less effective with your alien metabolism, but it should help give you some tiny advantage. Remember my proposal, now; think of it as a measure of revenge on you-know-who." He sauntered off, hissing a carefree rhythm.

"That whiteguard!" Harrumph croaked furiously, goggling his immense eyes at the Terran. "*Inth* is a mosst puissant alkaloid. Already I can feel a quickening along my gloob conduits. No telling what it will do to a non-Haterakan. How do you feel, Bully?"

"Never better, thanks." Retief lifted the keys from his pocket. "By the way, any idea what these might fit?" he asked.

Curiously, Harrumph examined the markings on the

crooked wires. "This one sseems to be ground-car key; an expensive model. I ssee it iss assigned slot in resserved lot." He singled out another key. "Thiss one, I believe, affordss entry into the private gaming chamberss known as Cassino of Miracless Incessantly Anticipated, three levels up. This one"—he indicated another—"represents membership in the Play-Toy Club, an arcane brotherhood devoted to titillating and then frustrating the reproductive urge. Their suite is in Q wing, top level." He fingered another key. "Thiss, I believe, openss a locker in the ssponssorss lounge, just below the reserved boxes." He emitted a hiss indicative of wondering admiration. "Owner of these iss *boulevardier* of firsst rank. May I assk"—he eyed Retief curioussly—"where you acquired them?"

"Oh, I found them in the pocket of an old suit," Retief said.

"Remarkable! I sshan't assk who wass wearing it." Harrumph handed the keys back to Retief, cocking his head toward the passage.

"I hear clank of accouterments," he said in a resigned voice. "Get ready, Bully. Thiss, as ssaying goess, iss it!"

6

A ten-Haterakan guard detail stood by as a boldy blazoned arena official unlocked the gate and waved the stars of the show out into the gloom of the passage. A plainly marked local posted there handed each of them an eight-foot wooden pole as they passed.

"One conssolation," Harrumph croaked, "it can't lasst long. Way I feel now, I couldn't outrun gravid ssplunt lizard."

"Don't try," Retief said. "Just stand up straight and look 'em in the eye."

Harrumph straightened his ruined tunic, tucked up the bedraggled braid of rank at his wrists, shouldered his staff. "Quite right, Bully," he said, freezing with an imperious glance a guard who had been about to prod him forward. "Now we will sshow rabble how heroess die."

Beyond the arch, the watery sun glared on the rippled surface of the water filming the arena. Side by side, Retief and the broken Haterakan officer strode boldly forward. As they emerged into view of the waiting spectators, an excited clacking and hissing broke out, ran across the stands.

"Ha! Hear how they exclaim," Harrumph grated. "But we sshall dissappoint their unwholessome lusstss for action by sstanding firm as monssterss charge down, thuss dying insstantly."

"That's the spirit," Retief said. "Let's take up our position right under the Admiral's box."

"As good a sspot as any," the other agreed. "And we'd besst get wiggle on. I ssee barrier rising, and dire-beasts are not noted for their reluctance to ssatiate their appetitess."

They had almost reached the appointed position when a deep-throated snort sounded from the shadows behind the now raised grid which had barred egress from the animal chute. A high-shouldered, long-legged creature resembling an oversized hyena with a bristling orange mane bounded into view. It ran in an awkward, shambing lope, following the line of the barrier wall. Halfway to the box where the trainers leaned forward eagerly, the animal checked, raised its wrinkled snout to test the air, then swung toward Retief and the cashiered Fleetmaster.

"I wass right," Harrumph said shakily. "Dire-beast it iss!"

As he spoke, the predator was splashing across the arena toward them at a purposeful canter, his head up, his daggerlike teeth bared.

"Steady, Harrumph," Retief called over the thunder of the crowd. "And don't give up hope until you find yourself looking at his bridgework from the inside." He reached into his pocket, took out one of the gas pellets he had removed from Rukktooey's gun, and crushed it under his nose.

2

For a moment, as the minty fragrance filled Retief's nostrils, nothing changed. The dire-beast broke into a full gallop, sending a spray of water high into the air. Then, abruptly, the swift uprush slowed, jelled into a gently drifting tracery of glittering droplets in which the reflected color of the sky faded from green to coppery red. Overhead, the cloud cover seemed to thin, became transparent, disappeared. The bright points of innumerable stars sprang up, glowing in rainbow hues, made visible via short-wave radiation. The long leap of the charging carnivore became a floating glide, which slowed into immobility while the avalanche of sound ran down to a rumble, died into utter silence.

Retief released his stave; it stood, suspended. Twenty feet away, the charging dire-beast poised, its forepaws, armed with nine-inch talons, clear of the ground, its large, greenish eyes half closed. Beside Retief, Harrumph posed, stiffly erect, staring with glittering eyes toward the unmoving tableau.

"Don't go away," Retief said. The words sounded muffled, distorted. The air was as thick as syrup on his tongue. He stepped past the Haterakan, plowing through the dense air as if through hip-deep mud, feeling the heat of friction scalding his skin. The film of water, set in static riffles, was as hard underfoot as ice.

He reached the guarded door under the VIP box; the sentries beside it stood like grotesqueries carved from polished hard-wood. He tried the elaborate latch. It resisted for a moment; then cracks opened in the tough plastic to which the hardware was mounted. Retief released the handle, already hot to his touch, stood back and watched the heavy metal fold and crumple as the entire assembly bulged from the door, bringing shards of the panel with it. Trailing chips, it traveled slowly past him on a flat trajectory.

He gripped the edge of the door, gave it a gentle tug, slid past its edge and stepped into a wide passage lined with doors. At the far end ruddy sunshine shone in through a fancifully arched and filigreed entrance. Beyond, on a wide terraced porte-cochere, a number of liveried doorkeepers stood frozen in the timeless poses of tip-ceremony around a long, glossy ground car, reaching for door handles, wielding superfluous whisk brooms, making ushering motions to a party of richly caparisoned patrons descending from the vehicle. Retief threaded his way among the group, taking care not to brush against them, looked the car over. It was, he decided, a trifle ostentatious, as well as being too large for maximum maneuverability. He went down the curving drive, fighting a tendency to float, stepped over a white-painted chain bordering a colorful fungus bed. The cars parked here in careless rows were obviously expensive models, bright with chrome and color, no two alike. Retief went along the line trying Rukktooey's keys, on the tenth try opened a low-slung two-seater parked near the exit gate. It was a custom export model of Gaspierre manufacture, fitted with metal-rod perches in place of seats. The gauges showed a full power charge.

Retief positioned himself at the front of the car, grasped the bumper carefully, and exerted a modest upward pull; then he went to the rear of the vehicle and repeated the maneuver. The weight slowly rose off the springs. When the tires were a foot above the pavement, he applied a light pressure against the side of the car, aligning it with the drive, then gave it a push toward the limousine entry. The motion was a little too abrupt; the bright red plastic dented under the pressure.

The car drifted out across the ornamental fungus, requiring a gentle upward thrust to keep it clear of the pavement. Retief walked ahead, gave the limousine blocking the way a shove, which sent it slowly gliding forward toward a plume bush, then guided the sportster into position directly in front of the doors and brought it down to earth, arresting its continued descent after the wheels were in contact, to avoid shattering the tires. Then he headed back to the arena.

As Retief passed back out through the broken door, he saw at a glance that the effects of the *inth* was beginning to wear off. All across the water-film, a faint stir indicated the return of visible movement.

He ran forward, skidded to a stop behind the dire-beast, now sliding forward in quickening motion. He caught the monster's scaly rattail, set himself, and heaved sideways. The appendage creaked, but held. Tugging hard, Retief eyed the stands like Babe Ruth picking the spot to place his next homer, swung the massive animal around, released it, saw it float away, rapidly gaining speed.

The deep, premonitory thrum of sound waves passing the audible frequency threshold had started up, was rising to a bass mutter, a growling rumble that became the full-throated crowd roar. Retief's feet sank through treacly water, splattering, as he leaped to Harrumph's side. Something whistled past him, struck the surface, bounded high: the smashed lock mechanism, completing its trajectory. He grabbed his stave, not yet toppled over, turned to see the dire-beast sliding away in a rising arc, to slam down full tilt into the Grand Admiral's box as sound returned to the arena like a giant clap of thunder.

"What—where—how . . . ?" Harrumph choked. "Bully—did you see that?"

"See what?" Retief inquired innocently.

"Just as you twitched—there wass gusst of wind! And dire-beast sseemed to halt in mid-sstride, whirl, and leap in one prodigious bound—there!" He pointed to the VIP box, where the aroused beast was tossing expensively enameled Haterakans left and right like jackstraws, howling furiously the while. Horns blew shrill blasts of alarm; metallically decorated cops appeared and, unable to shoot effectively because of the crowd, fired aimlessly into the air. Apoplectic livestock handlers swarmed about the scene of carnage, swinging power lariats and wielding electric prods in frantic attempts to control the rampaging carni-vore, as the band started up a brisk, discordant tune to cover the confusion.

"I've never been believer in poltergeisstss," Harrumph said shakily, "but in thiss case I'm going to make exception!" He stooped, came up with a fragment of door latch. "Look at thiss! It assailed passt me like chunk of sshrapnel!"

"I'm afraid the diversion didn't buy us much time," Retief said, indicating the barred door of a second animal chute hastily swinging open.

"They're russhing act little to distract cassh cusstomerss from accident," Harrumph said. "Now, indeed, we face end, Bully! It iss ssaid, bull-devil can take bite from hull plate, chew it up, and sspit out rivetss!"

"Don't despair," Retief called as the mob noise rose to a frenzy. "I'm working on arrangements for a way out of this—but before we make our break I think we need a little more activity in the wings to keep our hosts' attention occupied elsewhere."

"Arrangements? What arrangements?" Harrumph snorted. "Only arrangements we have time for now are extra twirl of prayer Yo-Yo—"

He broke off as from the shadows a massive form half the size of an Indian elephant paced forth, striped, fanged, tusked, hooved, bearing on its reptilian head a pair of yard-long chrome-bright horns.

"Right again," the ex-Fleetmaster said shakily. "Bully-devilss it iss..." A second great predator emerged as the first paused, swinging its head from side to side to bring first one eye, then the other, to bear on the scene. The second animal spotted the bait first. With a snuffling grunt, it shouldered its fellow aside and threw its enormous bulk into a swift canter that broke almost at once into a trot, then a full gallop, its hoofs raising a shower of spray as it bore down like a runaway switch engine on the two sacrifices. With a bellow, its mate followed. Quickly, Retief brought out another gas pellet, with a quick pinch, crushed the capsule, and drew a deep, minty breath...

3

The bull-devils plunged forward, looking as big as tyrannosaurs. Retief had a clear view of the gaping crocodile jaws and yawning purple throat of the nearest. And then the rush was slowing, turning into a drifting glide that stilled into movelessness as the sunlight shifted down the spectrum to a dusky red.

Retief walked forward, circled the immobilized colossi. At close range, they looked like hide-upholstered and spike-studded bulldozers. Working carefully to avoid breaking bones, he eased the brutes around, gently tugged them into motion toward the box in which Harrumph had pointed out the officials responsible for recreational planning. Then he crossed again to the now latchless door, took a ramp that led to the upper recreational levels of Q wing. The first few steps were heavy going; then he floated, guiding himself by using the handrail. At the top, he conducted a hasty reconnaissance of the warren of luxuriously decorated and furnished chambers filling this wing of the structure, before coming on the gambling rooms Harrumph had described. Rukktooey's key gave him entrance without the necessity for tearing the door down.

The casino had the half-familiar look common to all temples of chance, consisting of a series of gaudy, underlit salons fitted out with gaming devices ablink with colored lights, chrome fittings, and provocative levers, dials, and slots. A deluxe model Zoop tower occupied the place of honor in the first room; beyond it, Retief saw a Slam machine, a pair of Zintz tracks, the whirling spheres—now stationary—of a Blim-blim ring, and a vast roulette layout. There were a goodly number of gambling buffs in attendance, whom not even the show in progress in the arena a few hundred feet distant could woo from their obsession.

At the Zoop tower, a tense circle watched a pair of wagerers decorated in fashionable black and white zigzags who gripped the levers, their cranial spines erect in effort. With a sharp pull, Retief snapped the wires supporting the structure, atop which rested, he noted, a sizable pot in high-denomination chips. He gave the tower a delicate twist to impart a spinning motion, moved on to the next game.

Working briskly, Retief rotated the Slam cage into position so that its entire contents of thousand credit notes would cascade out through the opening, arranged the Zintz tracks to render inevitable an exciting combination play on the green and the pink, short-circuited the Blim-blim rig so as to ensure a thousand triple-XXX payoff, and stopped the roulette wheel with the little ball resting firmly in the tiny purple slot lettered, in traditional Old French, *maison pleincent,* which obligated the house to pay all bettors one hundred times their wager.

This accomplished, he left the casino, searched out the closely guarded door to the Play-Toy Club suite. Moving one of the armed entries carefully aside, he keyed the door, and was in a floridly decorated room, closely crowded by a numerous clientele distinguished by a somewhat furtive air, frozen in the act of eyeing the unpainted figures of smaller Haterakans, presumably the females of the species, indistinguishable from the males but for somewhat exaggerated chest-knobs, who posed among them offering trays of what appeared to be oversized toothpicks.

Retief inspected the dozen or so waitresses, selected two with exceptional chest-knob hypertrophy, and, with great caution so as to occasion no bruises, upended them gently toward the door.

With infinite care, he guided his trophies down the staircase. In the lower passage, he nursed the rigid bodies along to the locker rooms, guided the pair among the Haterakan gladiators frozen in the act of retouching or replacing their paint jobs, and erected them in a glassed stall lined with shower heads. There was a large four-spoked knob below the outlets; he gave it a deliberate half-turn, then hurried back out into the arena as the bull-devils, still hanging in air, somewhat askew but dead on course, had covered approximately half the distance to the stands. Retief carefully righted the rigid beasts, boosted them a foot or two to enable them to clear the barrier, and helped them on their way with an additional careful shove. Then he crossed at a brisk pace to the door from which the animals had emerged, followed a dark and narrow passage to a menagerie section lined with cages. All were empty with the exception of a large wire-meshed stall in which squatted a gaggle of foot-high, leathery gargoyles, complete with foot-long hooked beaks, tiny red eyes, and oversized feet from which clusters of talons sprang like bear-tooth necklaces.

Hastily, Retief stripped away the mesh, which broke up into patches like wet paper. Having effected an opening, he entered, gathered up six of the meat-hawks, and returned to the open air. He crossed to the detachment of police standing like brightly decorated marionettes by the gate, distributed the fowl, one to a customer, arranging one squatting atop a polished helmet, another perched on the tip of a rifle barrel, a third nestled on a noncom's folded arms...

A minute motion caught his eye as he completed the chore: one of the cops was visibly twitching a shredder, a motion normally quicker than the eye could follow. His time, Retief saw, was running out as the effect of the *inth* wore off. He ran to Harrumph's side, reached the Haterakan as sound returned to the arena with a crash.

"...thennn youu do have ssomething in mind " Harrumph was saying and broke off to gape at the hurtling form of the dire-beasts, lofting away in a large curve toward the fringed and tasseled VIP box.

"Let's go!" Retief snapped, and set off at a run for the broken door, before which a scene of riot burst into sudden violence as six bored policemen suddenly found themselves the collective object of the full attention of six voracious meat-hawks. As the unfortunate constabulary reeled in every direction, beating ineffectually at the rending talons and great cleaver-like beaks, the bull-devils arrived in the box above them with a rending smash and a yowl like a fire siren. No one offered interference as Retief dashed through the entry, Harrumph at his heels. From behind the locker-room doors, a chorus of clicks, clacks, hoots, and rumbles signaled a sudden excitement. The two fugitives had barely passed before the portals burst wide, disgorging a hopping, arm-flapping, bellowing horde of paintless Haterakans of both genders.

At the end of the corridor Retief bowled over a dignified Haterakan aristocrat blocking the door, sent a pair of doorkeepers spinning, leaped into the driver's seat of the sportster parked ready before the entrance. Off to one side, the bushes were still oscillating to the passage of the black limousine, now careening, driverless, across the lawn, headed for a reflecting pool. Harrumph tumbled over the side of the small car, righted himself as Retief started up and sent the compact vehicle hurtling down the drive. Behind them a lone shot rang out, scarcely audible above the rising tumult from the Recreation Complex. Glancing back, Retief saw windows burst from an upper story, and a shower of colorful chips spray out, followed by the head and shoulders of an obviously inebriated Haterakan who waved both arms, strewing credits to the wind, uttering shrill, joyous cries the while.

"What...what happened, Bully?" Harrumph choked, grabbing for support as Retief put the car through a set of four hairpin turns and shot up and over a high-arched, railless bridge.

"Tell you later," the Terran called back over the howl of the wind. "Right now I wish you'd give me directions to the port; and you'd better give your Yo-Yo a few spins and hope Rukktooey keeps his boat parked in a convenient location."

7

"It'ss incredible, Bully," Harrumph said for the fifth time, his immense eyes shining in the soft glow of the instrument panel of the stolen yacht in which they had made their dash for freedom. "Ssingle whiff of *inth* sshould have paralyzzed you. And as for thee...!" He rocked his head in a Haterakan gesture of amazement. "You Terriess are full of surprisses."

"You Haterakans aren't without your unplumbed depths, either," Retief pointed out. "Your remarks to the Grand Admiral on the phone just now showed a truly amazing command of Galactic invective."

"Ssubject insspired virtuosso performance," Harrumph replied fiercely. "Ahh... to think that I—Ssenior Fleetmasster of Archarch—sshould be tossed into ring with wild animalss like any pick-pouch or reticule-grabber! It iss inssult which can only be wiped out in vital juicess of perpetrator! Great will be my revenge, Bully!"

"We seem to be in the clear now." Retief scanned the screen, on which the last of the Haterakan planetary patrol vessels, hopelessly outpaced by the swift yacht, had now turned back. "Which brings us to the question of your plans for the future. Any particular place you'd like to be dropped off?"

"Dropped off? What'ss thiss, Bully? Are we not now palss in armss, brotherss in missfortune, twin victimss of injustice? Are we not to sstick together through fat and thin, gentleman adventurerss, drowning memoriess of misfortune in roisstering, kiki-fingering, recounting of colorful anecdotess to wondering yokelss of far placess?"

"Sounds like a fine program, Harrumph," Retief replied. "But I'm afraid I feel an obligation to warn the Blue Mooners what the Admiral has in mind for them—"

"Sso? Are you perhapss under impression I intend to miss prime opportunity to wipe eye of that rasscal Hikop? Ha! I can picture look on his emotion-reflecting members now, when desspissed nativess meet hiss sso-carefully elaborated sstrategiess with ssurprisse ambussh! Bessidess—by assissting in early defeat of thesse would-be clusster-conquerorss, I'll actually be ssaving cassualtiess in long run."

"A valid point. I'll set a course direct for Blue Moon."

"But don't misstake me, Bully," Harrumph amended. "I'll go along and lend a hand, but don't expect me to reveal any military ssecretss."

"I wouldn't think of it," Retief replied.

2

Ten hours later, Blue Moon was a misty azure disk swelling against the blazing backdrop of stars.

"How fortunate that you selected Rukktooey's personal transport," Harrumph muttered, eyeing the gathering units of the Haterakan fleet which showed on the screen as bright red blips ranged across their route. "And that Rukktooey engaged in smuggling operationss. Hiss anti-detection gear iss ssecond to none."

"Looks like the Admiral's a trifle overconfident," Retief commented. "I see only two major units; the rest are just gunboats."

"Hikop disslikess to damage hiss own prosspective property," Harrumph explained. "No point in bombarding ssurface into sea of molten lava, when sswift assault by landing partiess can accomplish dessired ressults."

Silently, the yacht hurtled onward, passing unnoticed through the loose cordon gathering at just over two A.U.'s from the target world, swept in past a pair of medium-sized satellites on which the wink of lonely lights indicated Terran settlements, dropped in across the night side of the planet, a vast sweep of darkness broken here and there by the glow of a small city.

Near the dusk line, a larger scattering of lights appeared. Retief flipped on the communicator, put out a call for approach instructions. His only reply was a crackle of static.

"Nothing on the standard navigation bands," he said. "If this is an indication of the state of affairs here, Hikop will have a picnic." He punched a key, activating the signal-seeking circuits. Almost at once, a voice was crackling through the small but luxuriously fitted flight deck of the yacht.

". . . course oh-three-five, range one-eighty! Pour on the coal, Maxie! Nail him before he knows what hit him!"

"Yeah, but maybe—" a more muffled voice came back, accompanied by a crackle of static.

"Maybe nothing! Sean's orders! Blast first and look for the dog tags later!"

"O.K.—if you say so, Les—but it's kind of a dirty trick, if he turns out to be the Fuller Brush man!"

"Bully—look!" Harrumph pointed to a new trace on the atmospheric screen—and at the same moment a strident blare sounded from the alarm screen.

"One away," the muffled voice crackled. "Two away, dead on course. . . ."

"Thought jusst occurred to me," the Haterakan blurted. "That it iss uss they're shooting at!"

Two livid blue lines were tracking swiftly across the screen, arrowing toward the doomed yacht. With a stroke, Retief cut all power, punched the big red-painted EJECTOR-ARM lever.

"Grab your hat, Harrumph," he snapped. "We're getting out!"

"But, Bully—I'm allergic to emergencies—!"

The Haterakan's protest was cut short by the sharp smack of the white EJECTOR FIRE lever as Retief slammed it home. In the next instant, with a tremendous *powww!* the deck tilted and spun as the entire flight compartment was blasted free of the ship. There was a second sharp impact, and a third. In the darkness of the flying capsule, Harrumph emitted a hoarse cry.

"Too late! They got us, the poacherss!"

"That was just the drag chutes opening," Retief called. He twisted to look overhead through the curving view screen in time to see a vivid flash which lit the interior of the escape capsule like a photoflood. A moment later, the metal walls leaped and rang like a gong as the shock wave passed. Then the sound: a rumbling *barooom!* resembling summer thunder.

"So much for Rukktooey's yacht," Retief said. "Now let's hope they don't bother sweeping up the crumbs."

3

On a promontory above a long sweep of blue meadow, Harrumph rubbed a bruised shin and eyed the amputated flight deck, lying canted sharply in the grass in the amber light of late afternoon.

"You and I sseem to have formed unpleassant habit of making crassh landingss, Bully," he grumbled. "One of us, in my opinion, iss jinxed."

"On the other hand, we seem to live through them, so maybe there's a counter-jinx working."

"Indeed I hope sso." Harrumph pointed across the valley. "Ssomeone iss coming—probably ssame ssomeoness who sshot us down."

"Two armored cars," Retief said, studying the vehicles approaching along a rutted track leading from a distant cluster of buildings. "Mounting infinite repeaters topside. Maybe these Blue Mooners aren't quite as unprepared as the Grand Admiral expects."

The two castaways watched as the lead car smoked up the hill, headed straight for them, a scarlet and gold pennant snapping from its prow.

"Do the rascals mean to run us down?" Harrumph barked. "I'll be grundled before I'll let thesse foreignerss ssee me sscuttle for ssafety."

At the last possible moment, the car swerved, skidded to a halt. The armored canopy popped up, and a man vaulted over the side, followed by a dozen others, carrying a variety of guns, mostly hunting weapons. They were a rough-looking crew but standing beside their leader, they looked by comparison like middle-aged bookkeepers.

The latter, standing with feet planted apart, fists cocked on hips, was seven feet tall, redheaded, square-jawed, with shoulders like a youthful Hercules. He was dressed in worn whipcord breeches, a khaki jacket, riding boots. Silently, he looked from Retief to Harrumph and back.

"Which one of you is the other one's prisoner?" he demanded in a resonant basso profundo.

"Neither," Retief said.

"What'd I tell you?" a man demanded, and yanked his gun clear of its holster, aimed it between the two new arrivals. "We been infiltrated!"

"We heard there was trouble brewing out this way," Retief said. "We came along to lend a hand."

"Don't listen to him, Sean," a thickset, bowlegged man said, pushing forward. He had a round face fringed with thin hair on top and stubble on the bottom. He chewed a cigar as he talked, fingering a blast pistol. "I guess we know a damned Hatrack when we see one—and a lousy renegade Terry—"

"Why don't you listen to what he's got to say?" a tall, blond man cut in. "Maybe we'd learn something."

"Suppose you explain that remark about trouble, Mister," the redhead rumbled. "There's gunners manning the hardware in both cars, in case you get ideas."

"He hass already told you, fellow!" Harrumph croaked. "We are here to thwart grandiose sschemess of Grand Admiral Hikop, due to arrive now at any moment!"

"You mean to stand here and listen to this here Lobster deliver a speech, Sean—while this spy pulls off whatever it is he's pulling off?" the dumpy man demanded.

"Shut up, Deucy. You talk, mister." Sean eyed Retief. "How come you're traveling with this enemy alien—and in a Hatrack boat, if that bird cage you've got instead of ac-chairs is any sign?"

Retief gave the redhead a brief outline of the events leading to the present confrontation.

"You claim the Lobsters are planning to jump *us?*" Sean said, frowning. He aimed a thumb at Harrumph. "And this fellow came along to help fight off his own friends and relations?"

"Watch your language!" Harrumph hissed. "I am ssworn enemy of malefactor Hikop! As for relationss, where were they in my hour of desperate need?"

"Don't listen to 'em, Sean," Deucy barked. "I got an idea this pair got wind of the legion, and—"

"Deucy, the next word out of you and you go sit in the car," the redhead cut him off. "You're spilling more than I'm finding out. Now..." He frowned darkly at Retief. "You say this Lobster admiral's planning a raid; I guess that means I'm supposed to sit tight and wait for him?"

"He's a decoy," a lantern-jawed man barked. "Sent in here to try to foul up the timetable!"

"What do you think, Lash?" Sean glanced at the clean-cut blond-haired man.

"If he's telling the truth," the other replied, "we're in trouble! We're not ready to stand off a full-scale attack!"

"Ha!" Deucy put in. "He come here to get all the dope on how we're organizing the Terran Defense Legion, and calling on all frontier worlds in the cluster to join in with men and supplies..."

The big man turned to face him. "Uh-huh," he said in a dangerous voice. "Anything else we should tell him?"

"Gee, Sean, I didn't...I mean, I won't..."

Silently, Sean hooked a thumb toward the car. Deucy muttered and took himself off. The blond man frowned at Retief. "You say there's an assault force massing off-planet. If that's the case, why haven't we picked up any signs of it on our long-range watch gear?"

"Becausse," Harrumph growled, "our   that iss, their vesselss are equipped with highly ssophissticated anti-detection insstallationss, dessigned precissely to foresstall disscovery by prosspective victimss!"

"They're crazy if they think they can pull it off," the big man grated. "We'll be ready for 'em!"

"The plan," Harrumph said, "iss to launch diverssionary attacks at one hundred widely disspersed pointss. Then, when your forcess, if any, have deployed to meet them   zormp! All unitss converge on sselected target, and beach-head is esstablished, after which heavily equipped ground forcess sspread out and ssweep defenderss into ssea!"

"Like that, eh?" Sean said thoughtfully. "In that case, our

play would be to hold back until they commit themselves. By the way, where does this Hikop plan to hit the beach with the real attack?"

"At place known as Port Ssapphire, on north coast of continent."

"Uh-huh," Sean nodded. "Simple enough—if true."

"Sean—you can see through this, can't you?" the lantern-jawed man spoke up. "If we hold our fire like this feller says, the Lobsters will wipe the floor with us—while we set on our hands!"

"And if he's *not* lying," Sean said, "and we move out to try to meet a dispersed attack—then their Sunday punch will go through us like a big toe through half-credit socks."

"I say shoot 'em now and then stand to our guns," a bald bartender-type with a red face piped up. "We can't afford to take no chances."

"Why not wait and see?" a firm feminine voice spoke up. A slim figure stepped through between a pair of heavy-weights who hastily began slicking down unruly hair and straightening soiled collars. The object of their tribute cast a cool green-eyed look at Retief, then turned to the big redhead.

"A man would have to be an idiot to come here on a spying mission with a member of the opposite camp," she said. "If what he says isn't true, we'll know soon enough."

"Now, Lisobel, stay out of this," Sean started.

The girl tossed her head. She had long, honey-blond hair, a classic jaw line, a short, straight nose. Her fine-arched brows rose in a look that suggested subterranean fires about to break loose.

"I'm already in it!" her voice crackled. "As much as any of you!" She whirled, pointing a slim finger at Retief. "This man may have risked his life to bring you this information! Aren't you even going to give him a chance?"

"Well, now, Lisobel—"

There was a stir from the rear; Sean turned, glad of the interruption.

"Lemme through there," a nasal voice snarled. The ranks parted and a man pushed through—a lean, hawk-nosed fellow with a bandaged arm and a swollen jaw. He turned a startled look on Retief.

"That's him!" he barked. "The one I was telling you about,

Sean! Him and the Lobster both! They're spies! Grab 'em quick!"

4

"Glad to see you made it, Lou," Retief said easily. "Where's Jack?"

"We got split up. Prob'ly the lousy Lobsters got him—thanks to you!" Lou turned to Sean, delivered his version of Retief's role in the loss of his boat and subsequent capture and escape.

"He had me fooled—for a while," he finished, "but I've got his number now!"

"If there's one thing I've got no use for," Sean said, turning to the man beside him, who silently handed over the shotgun, "it's a renegade Terry." He aimed the gun at Retief.

"All right, boys—take him!" he snapped. "He's got some questions to answer, so keep him in one piece!"

Two men stepped in confidently; Retief turned half sideways and struck out with both hands at once, landing a pair of solid chops that sent both men reeling back. He took a step to put his back to Harrumph's, gave the leader a cheerful grin.

"What's the matter, Sean, can't you do your own dirty work?"

Beside the redhead, Lou snarled, put his head down, and waded in. Retief met him with a solid left hook to the head, slammed a right to the pit of the stomach. Lou folded and fell on his face. A wild-eyed man with bushy black hair jumped over the fallen man, did a backflip as Retief uppercut him. More men, shouting now, swarmed in from left and right. Behind him, Retief sensed that Harrumph was smiting out valiantly.

"Hold on," Tolliver, the blond man, yelled. "Give them a chance... But his voice was lost in the uproar. A man dived at Retief from the side. He palmed him off, spun to meet two more plunging in, caught one by the collar and pitched him at the other's knees. Three men leaped in at once, met two haymakers and a knee to the stomach. Then a solid wall of yelling men rolled over Retief; six men grappled his legs, four more his arms, dragged him upright. Other men gripped Harrumph's arms and legs.

"Hey, Sean," a man called from the armored car parked

behind the group. "A TX from Cobolt Tower!" He leaned to twiddle dials on his field phone. An excited blat burst from it.

"...reinforcements! Just in from Jawbone, they say! Come out of noplace! Almighty big ships—two of 'em!"

A shot went up from the men. "...knew we'd get help!"

"So there's a Hatrack fleet just off-planet, eh?" Sean demanded sardonically over the hubbub. "Looks like they didn't slow our friends down any. I guess that's a good enough answer to your tale." He motioned the men back from around Retief and the Haterakan, raised the gun—

"Only a coward would shoot down an unarmed man in cold blood." Lisobel's voice cut clearly through the hubbub.

"For the love of Juniper," Sean roared, his face suddenly red. "I've got a war to run, girl! I can't waste time with a bleeding hearts club—"

"Heart which will bleed will be yours, large Terry," Harrumph cut in in his harsh voice. "Hikop iss crafty; he sseekss to ssucker you with thiss fiction of reinforcements! No Terry vessel could pass unchallenged through hiss blockade! And did your communicationss man himsself sstate theese new arrivals appeared with curiouss ssuddenness on his sscreenss? At closse range Haterakan concealment gear iss inoperative! Thuss the Grand Admiral hopess to give himsself a few added minutess of ssurprisse!"

"Maybe you'd better play it safe, Sean," Retief said. "Run an intercept on these alleged Jawboners, before they hit atmosphere."

"I can't," the redhead growled. "With Lou's boat gone, I've got nothing with combat capability but atmosphere craft!"

"In that case, you'd better get them in the air in a hurry. Hikop will carry his masquerade as far as he can. By the time your radar can recognize that those are Haterakan carriers, the bombs will already be on the way."

"I've got no fuel to waste, blast you! The more you talk the more I don't know which way to jump! Until I see evidence that those are enemy vessels, I've got to assume they're what they claim to be!" Sean made a savage motion with his hand. "All right, don't stand around with your mouths open," he bellowed at his men. "We'll have to stand by until they tip their hand! We've got no choice!"

"What about this pair?" A small man with bat ears waved his

gun at Retief and Harrumph.

"We'll lock 'em up until we know which way things are running." Sean shot a hot look at the girl. "And if they've lied to me, I'll personally trim 'em into cut bait and feed 'em to the grass crabs!"

5

The makeshift prison to which the prisoners were escorted was a tumble-down former barn built of stone and massive timbers, manned by a lean, white-haired oldster with a weather-beaten face and snapping blue eyes.

"Howdy, Miss Lisobel," he greeted the girl who had accompanied the detachment. "Who's this fellow?" he demanded, looking Retief over. "Don't remember seeing him around here before." He looked Harrumph up and down. "And a Hatrack. Where'd you get him?"

"They crash-landed, Jimmy," the girl said. "Sean wants them guarded until he can check their story."

"They come snooping around, Harvey—" the bat-eared man started.

"That's Sergeant Major Harvey to you, boy, for the duration," the old fellow barked. "Guarded, hey? O.K. Get 'em inside here. If you weekend heroes had the wits of the wood-weevils that are rattling around where your brains ought to be, you'd know better than to bunch up where one enemy ping-bomb could take out the bunch of you!"

"Heck, Harvey—I mean Sarge—there ain't no Lobsters inside o' six parsecs—"

"A lot you know! I been telling you sack-sailors you're overconfident! Now skedaddle! I'll take care of this pair!" The jailor hefted an immense antique revolver.

"Watch it, Harvey. These are dangerous spies—"

All heads turned to look upward as a brilliant white star lit the scene suddenly, etching upturned faces in stark black and white. Across the sky, a white streak elongated like chalk across a blackboard, fading to harsh yellow, cherry red, then dying, leaving a fading trail of glowing dust behind it. A second streak arched across the sky, fading, dying.

"Ye gods!" someone yelled. "Those babies are in some kind

of hurry! Must of burned off a ton of hull metal apiece, that time!"

"Grand Admiral iss ahead of sschedule," Harrumph croaked. "Those vesselss are not over one hundred miless out now, on first braking-pass!"

"We better get back!" the bat-eared man said. "If them *ain't* Jawboners, we got a problem!"

"All right, you spy-catchers can leave the pris'ners to me." Harvey stood grimly by as the escort hurried away into the gathering dusk.

"Spies, eh?" He locked the stout door with a big iron key, looking Retief over. "Looks like you picked funny company to travel in, sure enough—but what's your side of it feller?"

"We got wind of an attack and dropped in to help out." Retief said. "Sean seemed to think we're on the other side. Maybe it's the bad light."

The old man grunted. "Sean's a good man," he said. "But he's under a lot of pressure right now. How'd you happen to find out about the attack?"

"We had the pleasure of being questioned by Admiral Hikop. He did a little bragging."

"You say 'we'; you mean to say this here Hatrack's throwed in with us Terries?"

"Sshort ssession on torture rackss wass ssufficient to sway my allegiance to any force opposssing wretched Hikop!" Harrumph explained. "But at time I did not ssusspect our reception would be characterized by ssuch idiocy as hass been thuss far dissplayed."

Harvey looked keenly at Retief. "Seems like Lisobel likes your looks. And she ain't often wrong. And you don't look to me like no spy, son. Are you?"

"Not this time, Sergeant Major."

"Kind of a tight spot fer Sean," the old fellow mused. "If he believes you and holds back his planes   and you're lying   he's had it."

"He's still got time to scramble his squadrons and get in position to interdict the strike at Port Sapphire," Retief said. "But not if he waits much longer."

"And if he don't believe you, and spreads 'em   and you *ain't* lying—he's had it even worse." Harvey cocked his head. "You wouldn't by any chance have any proof o' your story?"

"Just words, Sergeant Major. No evidence. Someone will have to go upstairs for that, I'm afraid."

"Hmmm. And all the interceptors Sean could scrounge up—everything from obsolete V-90's and Norge Irrompibiles that have been bush-hopping for the last twenty years, to a brand new K-ooo high-altitude fighter are setting on the runway a few hundred yards from here. They'd be sitting ducks for a quick sneak punch."

"Uhhuh. Sean's conserving fuel, it seems, until he can make a definite radar identification."

"What radar?" Harvey snorted. "Hell, son, we're operating on a worn-out shoestring! So far all Sean's got is a lot of talk and big ideas! He's tried to line up all the worlds around these parts—Blackstrap, Busted Axle, Saddlesore, Mule Kick, Outpost, Jawbone—but so far all he's got is excuses. Seems like they ain't convinced there's a war on."

"No long-range ID radar?" Harrumph inquired. "In that case, gentlemen, you may sscratch one planet. Hikop will bring hiss units to ground unopposed, and firsst thing localss will know of their error will be impact of artillery sshells in their midst!"

"Tough on Sean." The oldster shook his head. "Times like this the man in charge is carrying quite a load, all those decisions to make . . ." He looked at Retief. "Funny thing," he said. "I'm getting old, I guess. Careless. Like now; I feel myself going to sleep on my feet, and the key to the door laying right there on the desk." He sat down on the chair, laid the pistol aside, leaned back, closed his rheumy eyes.

"Guard out on the line's a right nice boy," he said. "Wouldn't like to see him get hurt." He opened one eye. "Be kind of a nice gesture if yer Hatrack friend was to stay here. Kind of a token o' good faith."

"I'm sure he'd want it just that way," Retief said. "Sleep tight, Sergeant Major. I think there's still time to turn up a convincing souvenir."

6

A startled plane guard jumped up as Retief came up to the long, sleek ship, parked nose-into-the-wind at the side of the sandy strip.

"Substitute pilot," Retief said briefly as the young fellow swung his gun around uncertainly. "Just unchock those wheels, will you?"

He swung up into the cockpit, strapped in, with a touch of the starter button started the fifty megahorse engine. Retief gunned the ship, swung out into the runway, taxied to the downwind end. From the direction of the Operations tent, there was a wink of pink light; a shot whickered close enough to hear even over the thunder of the jet. Then the craft was racing forward, lifting, its nose pointed to the stars.

Five minutes later, at ninety thousand feet, Retief picked up the first faint pulse on his radar. In the dim cockpit light, he switched on the chart, watched the landscape unroll with the red dot that represented his aircraft centered on the ten-inch screen. Forty miles to the west was the dark blob of the coastal town near which the Haterakans proposed to land en masse. Far above, at extreme range, the twin blimps of the Haterakan carriers danced on the screen, decelerating rapidly now as they took up the stations from which they would launch their landing craft.

Retief flipped keys, setting up the course vector for an intercept on automatic pilot. The acceleration pressed him back in his seat as the eager craft surged forward. He switched his communicator to command channel.

". . . you in the stolen plane," Sean's voice roared. "You've got to land sometime—and when you do—"

"Keep your eyes peeled, Sean," Retief cut in. "Watch the lead ship."

"You!" Sean yelled. "I don't know what in the name of nine devils you think you're doing, but break it off! That's an order! Bring that aircraft back here in one piece or—"

"Better you order a red alert, effective now, Sean," Retief interrupted the tirade. "If everything works out, I think you'll want to scramble your squadron in a hurry a few minutes from now."

"What are you talking about, you—you horsethief! That's my best fighter you've got there—all I've got to stand the enemy off with, until our allies come through—"

"Sure. And I'd hate to see you lose it on the ground."

"Listen! I'm tracking you on an intercept course with that Jawbone transport! What crazy stunt are you planning?"

"If she's a Jawbone transport, I'll write 'I was a bad boy' on the blackboard a hundred times. If not..."

"Hey—if that tub *is* a Lobster man 'o war, he'll blast you out of the sky! I can't afford to lose my K-three-oh! Break it off and get out of there!"

"If he nails me, it will be a convincing demonstration of what I've been telling you," Retief came back. "Let's wait and see how it turns out. I'll have to go now, Sean. I'm going to be busy for the next five minutes."

At full emergency intercept speed, Retief raced forward, watching the incoming vessel as it dropped deeper into the planetary atmosphere. He switched his gunnery screen to high mag; the enemy was descending fast from an altitude of forty miles. Second by second, Retief closed in; when he ranged the vessel at a scant twenty miles, the spaceship abruptly altered course toward him. An instant later, the tiny traces of air-to-air missiles lanced out. He held his fire, watched as the proximity dial swept from fifteen miles to ten, to five—

When it seemed the projectiles were almost in his cockpit, he put the K-ooo on its back and dropped away in a vertical dive. There was a sharp *whap!-whap!* as the missiles, unable to follow the abrupt course alteration, detonated harmlessly far astern of their elusive target.

"You up there—I saw two heavy K's blow just now!" Sean's excited voice burst from the panel. "Are you...did you...?"

"You'll be relieved to know I'm O.K., Sean," Retief came back cheerily. "His aim was wild. Hold tight, now..."

"Wait a minute, you! You're right on top of him! You're not crazy enough to try to ram the son of a flagpole?"

"Does that mean you're convinced? Stand by and I'll see if I can't clinch my argument."

"I told you to break off and bring that aircraft back to base, blast you! If he's a Jawboner, like he said, you're wasting fuel! And if he isn't—you're wasting an interceptor!" As Sean raved on, Retief brought his ship around in a rising curve toward the monster vessel, now no more than three miles distant. He switched off the screens, doused the cockpit lights, stared out through the canopy for visual contact—and saw the great ship, a quarter-mile cigar-shape typical of Haterakan design slanting away from him, reaching for maneuvering space after the surprising failure of its missile launch.

"All right, all right! I'm convinced!" Sean yelled. "I can see him running—I don't know why, but no honest ship would do that! Now get out of there before he swats my airplane!"

"I can't afford to, now," Retief replied. "I'm inside his screens. If I stick close enough, he can't use his heavy stuff on me. That gives me a slight advantage."

Steadily, he closed the gap, as the fleeing Haterakan ship, hampered by the unaccustomed drag of atmosphere and planetary gravity, sought to outdistance him, gain the relative safety of the troposphere, from which it could launch a new and irresistible attack. Its sister ship, a hundred miles to the west, was changing course, its trace on the screen curving to join her ally.

At a distance of little over a mile, the giant Haterakan carrier angled sharply upward in a desperate bid to shake off the perplexingly persistent midget which had eluded her salvo—the opportunity Retief had waited for. His swift craft raced in, coasting up past its normal operational ceiling. At a range of half a mile, Retief slammed the FIRE switch home. The aircraft grunted and lurched as its entire battery of rockets, explosive projectiles, and heat-seeking ballistic torpedoes sprang away in one massive volley aimed at the giant's vulnerable hull. As Retief flipped the interceptor on its back and rolled under and away from the invader, a glint of red light flashed along the plane's polished prow. The shock wave struck, slammed the light craft into a wildly slewing roll. Retief righted it, looked back. Far above the astern, a great white fire blazed in the sky, raining flaming wreckage in a mile-wide swath.

"Ho-ly jump-ing Jeremy!" Sean's voice crackled, almost lost in the static generated by the boiling holocaust. "I can see the fireball from here! It looked like you flew that K-three-oh right into her stern tubes!"

Retief watched as the disintegrating carrier fell past him, the tiny lights of escaping parasite craft streaming away from the hulk like sparks from a burning brand.

"She's laid her eggs, Sean," Retief called over the background crackle and roar. "Looks like about fifty of them got away." Below, he saw a splash of light as the carrier struck.

". . . orders!" Sean was shouting to someone. "Scramble and orbit! Indigo Bay will have to take its chances, and so will Aquamarine and Azure Hills and fifty other towns! I don't care what you've picked up on your screens! We're laying for them at Port Sapphire, just like the man said!" His tone changed.

"You, there—whatever your name is—on the borrowed plane! I wanted proof. I guess I got it! If you'd like to take up station with me and my bunch, we'll see how many of these babies we can rack up before they get tired and go home!"

8

In the long, sagging tent that was Operational Headquarters of the Terran Defense Legion, Sean and his jubilant men stood around the primitive potbellied electric stove, quaffing great mugs of hot coffee and slapping each other on the back.

"It was one of those decisive actions that decides the whole course of a war," Sean stated exultantly. "It's like Marathon, and the Alamo, and the stand at Wolfgang's World! We stopped 'em in their tracks and sent 'em running for home! Seven Lobster assault boats blasted, and ten more captured intact, and a stockade full of Hatrack prisoners! But by the nine tails of the Fire Devil, Bully, without your inside dope on their battle plan, they'd have smashed us flat!"

"Your fighter pilots had a bit to do with the victory," Retief pointed out, lighting up a Jorgenson cigar. "But the Haterakans aren't beaten, Sean, just discouraged for the moment."

"So what? Let 'em try us again! I guess we can handle anything a bunch of Lobsters can throw at us, and pay it back with interest!"

"Kindly remember that there are Lobssterss and Lobssteress, my dear Ssean," Harrumph said in an irritable growl. "You will recall that I alsso wass inssstrumental in bringing newss of Hikop's intent—though I confess that my friend Mr. West'ss insspired intervention wass the masster sstroke of the affair!"

"I never seen anything like it, Sean," a bristly-jawed man grinned, showing teeth that had patently failed to see their dentist twice a year. "Once them babies seen we was ready for 'em, they couldn't give up quick enough!"

"Naturally," Harrumph spoke up. "Why sshould they get themsselvess killed carrying out operation Grand Admiral had assured them would be child'ss play?"

"You go in for some fancy demonstrations, Bully." Sean grinned at Retief. "You dropped that carrier right in the front yard." He delivered a ringing kick to a large, heat-curled section of hull plating salvaged from the downed heavyweight. "I can't read Lobster," he said, indicating the curlicued symbols etched in scorched paint across the trophy. "But I knew Haterak sheet metal when I saw it. Damn near hit me on the head!" He turned to Harrumph. "What's it say anyway?"

"'Authorissed Perssonel only,'" the Haterakan interpreted.

A roar of laughter greeted the translation.

"That's as good a battle cry as any," Sean announced. "And we'll show these blasted Hatracks what it means, too, present company excepted." He took a gulp of coffee. "That's our Legion motto from now on, boys! We'll post it on every world on the frontier before we're done!"

"Why not let the CDT handle it from this point on?" Retief inquired.

In the background, an atonal twanging had started up, inspiring a number of the men to join in a hearty rendition of "Gonna Dig a Big Ditch around Texas."* Sean winced and leaned closer. "When the Haterakans first started nosing around our worlds, we paid 'em no mind," he said grimly. "First thing we knew, they'd set up fueling stations right under our noses—on our own satellites! Claimed we weren't using 'em and they had as much right as anybody. We called in the CDT—and got brushed off like a Sunday suit. Then the Lobsters got bolder, took to buzzing our towns, blanketing our communications,

---

*Copyright 2940 by FOMU Corp.

interfering with shipping. We tried the CDT again and got told we were troublemakers. Then the E.T.'s came out in the open, took over Blackstrap's outer moon, and kicked the water miners off—and I knew it was time to do something. I got a few men together, set up shop here on Blue Moon and started scrounging whatever equipment I could get my hands on—"

"According to rumor, you've been pretty busy at that last chore," Retief said mildly. "I understand half the shipping on the frontier has been hit. Where do you keep all the loot?"

Sean looked surprised. "Hell, Bully—how much do you think I could do with one thousand-tonner? I had exactly one fast, space-worthy boat—the one the Hatracks blasted out from under Lou and Jack. Their orders were to collect arms any kind of arms—anyplace they could get 'em! Maybe they got overeager and collected a little cash along with the guns on the theory it might come in handy for buying a shipment out-cluster and sneaking it in past the CDT. But that's all! We never touched any inter-planet shipping, or raided any settlements!"

"Besst you defer hisstorical ressume until later," Harrumph said. "If I know Grand Admiral, he iss even now raging about deckss of hiss flagsship, disspatching orderss in all directionss for massive concentration of forcess for next attempt. The Admiral disslikess being frusstrated in hiss little whimss."

"You figure this Hikop'll try it again?" Sean frowned.

"You may depend upon it," the alien croaked. "Having once been thwarted in hiss object, he will return to affray with renewed intenssity! Ssuch iss nature of hiss fanaticissm!"

"What do you think, Bully?"

"Why you asking him?" Lou demanded. "I still don't trust him any farther than I can pitch a pack mule!"

"That's 'cause you're about half smart," Harvey spoke up. "And it's the wrong half."

"Take it easy, Lou," Tolliver put in good-naturedly, "As Sean says—Mr. West has presented his credentials."

"Huh! Could of been just a grandstand play, a put-up job—"

"Nonssensse!" Harrumph cut him off. "Grand Admiral Hikop iss not Lobster to wasste sship of line merely to penetrate headquarters of what he considerss nesst of sspoils-sportss!"

"What I'd like to know is," a scar-faced man named Cecil spoke up, "how'd that Hatrack admiral know to hit Blue Moon in the first place?" He eyed Retief. "There's lots of places he could've jumped but he picked Legion Headquarters."

"Telling point," Harrumph answered for him. "Hikop'ss intelligence apparatuss hass obviously penetrated your headquarterss, friend Ssean!"

"Yeah—and I could tell you how," Lou muttered.

"Nuts, Lou," Cecil said. "These fellers wasn't even here then—"

"Then you tell me—"

"How do I know?"

"All right, quiet down, you jaspers!" Sean cut through the babble.

"Harrumph is right," Retief said. "Hikop thought he'd pick Blue Moon off without any trouble; he's based a whole campaign on the idea. He can't give up now without dropping his whole grand scheme of conquest."

Sean looked suddenly grim.

"You think he means to take over the whole cluster, eh, Bully?"

"Anybody'd think this saddle tramp was a lifelong pal o' yours," Lou said loudly. "Why don't you ask me what I think? Now, my idea is—"

"I'm asking Bully West, that's why!" Sean bellowed, his face redder than usual.

"He's not even a member of the Legion!" Lou yelled back.

"Oh, yeah? Well, he is now! In fact, as of tonight, he's a captain! George!" Sean whirled to a large, bowlegged man. "Lend me a set of captain's bars!"

George offered a tarnished set of tracks from his hip pocket. Sean pinned them to Retief's collar.

"There!" he said. "Now he outranks you forty ways from Sunday, Lou—so keep your trap shut, and say 'sir' when you do it! Now..." He addressed Retief. "Maybe you and me and Tolliver better get busy doing some planning, Bully, before the Hatracks have time to hit us with the second wave."

"I was thinking along other lines, Sean," Retief said, drawing on his cigar. "I believe the Haterakans have kicked out some Terry miners and set up an outpost on one of the moons of Blackstrap, not far from here..."

"You don't mean you think we ought to go over there and talk truce?" Sean sounded shocked.

"By no means," Retief said coolly. "Now's the time to counterattack."

2

"Admiral Hikop holds Blackstrap Ssatellite with minimal forcess," Harrumph stated positively after the discussion had proceeded to details. "At thiss moment he will have drawn off all available personnel in preparation for a renewed assault here. A determined sstrike ussing hiss own captured sshipss might well ssucceed in dislodging hiss foothold."

"It could work." Sean smacked his palm with his fist in a familiar gesture. "I've got men enough to man those tubs—and Harrumph here can give us a fast run-down on combat operation—"

"Mr. Wesst iss also checked out on this model," Harrumph put in. "Now I suggest we wasste no more time in idle chatter. The ssole hope of ssucess liess in sswift, decissive action!"

"You're right!" Sean turned to the others, listening open-mouthed. "You heard it, boys! Tolliver, you pick the volunteers: twenty-five men to a pogo stick—and you've got one hour to get 'em shipshape and combat-ready!"

"Count me in, Tolliver," Lisobel spoke up.

"What's that?" Sean arched a rust-red eyebrow. "Listen, girl, this is a combat operation!"

"I can handle a tracking panel as well as any man here!" The girl's green eyes flashed. "You don't think I came this far just to be parked with the baggage, do you?"

Sean hesitated. "All right," he nodded. "You're on!" He whirled to Tolliver. "Roll 'em, Lash. We lift out of here in fifty-nine minutes—and we'll hit those Lobsters with a surprise that'll turn their head-quills white overnight!"

3

It was a twelve-hour run at fleet cruise velocities to the Blackstrap system. The improvised Terran task force—nine captive vessels had been successfully launched for the effort—encountered two enemy pickets en route, but each time Harrumph satisfied their challenge with a rapid string of bogus operational orders.

The Haterakan-occupied moon—the most distant satellite of Blackstrap, itself a sparsely populated, oversized world lying barely within its sun's habitable zone—swelled on the lead ship's screens, a frosty white, slightly misshapen sphere, a bare five hundred miles in diameter.

"Not much to it," Sean said grimly. "But it was Terry territory, by Hector, and with a little luck it will be again!"

At the communicator, Harrumph barked and hooted in reply to anxious queries rising from the station below.

"They are growing ssusspiciouss," he announced, looking up from the screen, so arranged that only his own Haterakan visage was visible to the ground station. "Thiss chap wisshess to know why we're coming thiss way when he personally heard fleet orderss directing all units *that* way."

"Tell him we need to fuel up and take on supplies," Sean directed.

After another exchange of excited gutterals, Harrumph relayed the reply: "He sstatess that he hass had no insstructionss to ssupply any tail-end Charliess sshowing up five hourss late for grand assemblage of fleet. He further advissess that he iss engaged in taking hiss ssemi-quarterly inventory, and hass no intention of loussing up hiss recordss jusst to ssuit platoon of gold-bricking ten o'clock sscholarss. There'ss more, but it sscarce bearss repeating."

"Stall him for another five minutes," Sean snapped. "Then he can yell his head off." He directed the slim, sleek vessel into a close tangential approach orbit designed to use the planetoid's feeble gravitational attraction to the maximum for braking from interplanetary velocity.

"Poor fellow iss deeply dissturbed by our failure to ssheer off," Harrumph relayed after a particularly virulent stream of croaks and clicks had issued from the screen. "He threatenss to report uss in quadruplicate to Grand Admiral himsself, for failure to ssubmit proper paper work ssix weekss in advance."

"Tell him I'll explain the whole thing to him in easy-to-understand terms in about another ten minutes," Sean suggested. "Hold tight, all hands! I'm standing this bucket on her tail..."

The buffeting of retrojets drowned all conversation for the next quarter hour. At an altitude of five miles above the rocky, magma-lumped surface of the airless worldlet, Sean brought the little vessel into approach attitude, waited until his eight wingmen had reassembled astern, then set his course, and raced over the curve of the close horizon for the Haterak station.

No hostile ships rose to meet the Terrans as they swept low over the scattering of squat sheet-metal buildings near the tailings of the abandoned mining operation. Unopposed, they grounded a quarter of a mile from the hemi-cyclindrical structure which Harrumph assured Sean housed the offices of the base commandant. In utter stillness, the space-suited men broke out the ground assault cars, formed up in a flying wedge, and advanced. Not a gun was fired as they converged on the target area, dismounted, and with ready blast rifles covered the last fifty yards on foot. Sean fired a bolt into the door, kicked it wide and led the invaders into the station. As he aimed his gun at a closed inner lock door, Retief put out a restraining hand.

"Let's try the latch," he suggested. "We may want to get out of these suits ourselves after a while." He opened the door and stepped through. A Haterakan, wearing silver quills and sporting an orange and green paint job indicative of medium high rank, but with his braided tunic hanging open carelessly, jumped up from a pink-glowing screen from which an elaborately plumed and enameled Haterakan countenance stared forth, cut off in mid-sentence by the interruption.

"Hold your fire, boys." Sean covered the alien with his rifle. "Harrumph, tell him to play   th and he won't get hurt."

Harrumph stepped forward,   soothingly to the officer, who waggled his head in silent assent. A sharp exclamation broke from the watching face on the screen.

"Ah, it's Colonel-General Burrapp himmself." Harrumph executed a sardonic bow to the glowering visage, following up with a string of Haterakan polysyllables. The Colonel-General emitted a sound like a short in a ten-megavolt circuit and blanked the screen.

"Now he knows," Harrumph announced in a satisfied tone. "My dear Terries, if you could have grassped import of poor

Burapp'ss remarkss, you would have felt well repaid for your efforts!"

"Ask this fellow where the rest of the station personnel are!" Sean snapped.

"He iss all," the Haterakan announced after a short exchange. "There iss no one elsse."

"You mean...?" Sean looked from the alien to Retief and back. "That's all there is to it?"

'So it seems," Retief said. "Congratulations, Colonel."

"I just promoted myself to general," Sean cried cheerfully. "That makes you a colonel, Bully. What the hell, promotions for everybody! I guess we earned 'em! The first piece of Terry soil recaptured—but it won't be the last!"

"Hey!" a man called from a doorway leading into another room. "Looky here! A warehouse, stacked chock-full! Winter gear, dope-sticks, fuel, chow—the works!"

"Hot dog!" Another stepped through, reappeared with a braid-encrusted Haterakan tunic draped over his leather jacket. "How do I look, boys?"

As the invading troops spread out to check the loot, Sean turned to Retief, a grin spreading from ear to ear.

"If this is what the invading business is like," he said happily, "I think I might get to like it!"

4

Twelve hours later, lavishly supplied with food, ammunition, armaments, captured tri-D tapes and enough gold braid and varicolored ribbon to adorn a county fairgrounds, the victorious troops descended to Blackstrap, leaving a forty-man garrison to hold the recaptured moon station against all comers.

"They will have no trouble, General Braze," Harrumph assured the big redhead. "Admiral Hikop ssharess Haterakan idiossyncrasy which occasionss profound disstaste for charging into muzzles of one'ss own gunss."

"We'll stir up some support from these plowboys now," Sean stated definitely. "And if they're a little slow about contributing, we're in a spot now to do more than beg. I'll parlay these nine pogo sticks into a fighting force that will blast a hole all the way through to the Archarch's palace at Haterak!"

5

Two hours after landing, to the accompaniment of a stirring call to arms broadcast planet-wide as the tiny force barreled in through Blackstrap's frosty atmosphere, the Terran Defense Legion had established itself in new headquarters in a baronial farmhouse featuring a vast dining hall, hand-hewn ironwood beams, a fireplace accomodating ten-foot logs, and a well-stocked ale cellar.

"Sso far my revenge on perfidious Hikop proceedss well," Harrumph remarked to Retief, chafing his anterior chelae together with a tooth-loosening sound. "If General Braze iss correct in hiss esstimate of number of eager volunteerss who will flock to colorss now that he hass ssuccess to sshow, I may well have pleasure of perssonally garroting sscoundrel before firsst snow fliess!"

"So far, fortune smiles on the Legion," Retief assented. "Militarily it doesn't amount to much, but it might help the CDT see the situation in a new light."

"By way, where iss hiss Excellency?" Harrumph inquired, gazing about the long room. "He dissappeared half hour ssince..."

There were sudden exclamations from the direction of arched doorway leading to the interior of the house.

"Wow!" someone yelled. "Lookit the chief!"

All heads turned as a resplendent figure appeared in the doorway, surveyed the room with the look of a Roman emperor arriving for his coronation. Sean's plain khaki bush jacket and scuffed boots were gone. Now his broad shoulder strained the royal blue polyon of a masterfully cut tunic splashed with jeweled decorations. Gold braid ran down the seams of tight-fitting dark blue breeches like rivulets of fire. His boots were mirror-polished, fitted with jeweled platinum spurs. The holster buckled to his hip was mounted with gold and rubies, though the well-worn butt of his standard Concordiat service model blast pistol still protruded from it. He planted his feet like an admiral weathering high seas, flourished a long cigar in casual salutation to his astounded audience.

"Thought I'd better doll up a little," he explained airily. "Les used to be a tailor before he joined up. Not bad, eh?"

"Good night, Sean," a leathery-faced fellow blurted. "You look like a fifty-credit joy girl on the way to a bankers' convention!"

"That's General Braze to you, Homer!" Sean pointed the cigar at the man. "And don't you forget it! Sure, it's a little fancy—but when the volunteers start pouring in, they'll expect to see somebody that looks like a winner, not a backwoods lumberbum with a greasy collar! Now, the rest of you get busy and rustle up some snappy-looking uniforms. Lash, issue 'em two medals per man. We've got enough gewgaws and hardware to dress up the Swiss Navy!"

"What navy's that?" Homer scratched behind his ear.

"I don't know—but I hear they were sharp dressers! Now everybody turn to! This is a big day for the Legion—and I'm declaring it a holiday! I've already sent word out for some cooks to roast up a pair of heifers with all the fixings, and there's enough booze on hand to float a ferryboat! This is our night to howl, and I challenge any man in the house to outdrink, outeat, or outtalk me!"

In the roar that went up. Sean looked across the room at Retief and winked.

"I wonder," Harrumph said thoughtfully, "if early ssuccess iss not going to our general'ss head?"

"Maybe," Retief said. "Let's hope he's got broad enough shoulders to hold up the load."

6

It was close to midnight when the last of the feasters pushed back his plate, loosened his belt, belched, and prepared to settle down to some serious drinking.

"What's eating you, Lash?" Sean boomed to his second-in-command, sitting silent across the table from him. "You look like you just heard from your mother-in-law."

"It's nothing; I'm just a little surprised. I thought we'd have a couple of hundred new recruits by now. At last count we had two: a twelve-year-old boy and his grandfather."

"Patience, Lassh," Harrumph croaked. "As ssoon as word sspreadss of general'ss coup in recovering ssatellite, thousandss will bessiege him for place in rankss of conquerorss!"

"Ha! That's right, Rumpy old boy!" Sean turned to two well-lubricated warriors who were clumsily lifting a crimson banner, blazoned in gold with the device derived from the fallen Haterakan carrier, to a position above the fireplace.

"Hey—you there, McGillicuddy and Snarkovicz!" he bellowed. "Hoist it up a little higher where we can all see it! We'll give 'em something to rally to!" He grinned at Retief, tried to slap him on the back, almost fell from the chair. He raised a quart-capacity mug in salute to Harrumph with such vigor that ale slopped out and splattered across the shirt front of Lou, seated beside Tolliver, glowering.

"And thanks to you, too, you boiler-plated son of a Quonset hut! You're all right!"

Harrumph cocked his shredders in an expression of wry tolerance and turned to Lou.

"Are you *ssure* we haven't met somewhere—before the encounter aboard my sship, I mean? Possibly lasst year on Croanie...?"

"No, you overgrown crawfish!" Lou barked and swiveled away from the Haterakan. "Lay off bugging me or so help me I'll twist your head around so far you can look down the back of your neck!"

"Hey—watch your mouth, Lou," Sean boomed. "Harrumph's an ally of ours—"

"It ain't right!" Lou barked back, "An enemy alien with his feet—all four of 'em—under our table, while we're fighting a war with his kinfolks!"

"He already told you he's no friend of this Hikop that's causing all the static. Now leave him be, or I'll be the one doing some neck-twisting!"

"Hey, uh, General," a burly man with a bald head spoke up. "How much longer you and your army going to be hanging around my place here? I got spring crops to set, wood to cut, and a barn roof needs fixing—"

"Relax, friend," Sean grunted. "The boys just bought your satellite back for you! I hope you're not grudging 'em a little party!"

"It's nothing to me who owns that rock," the farmer protested. "And that's my next year's beer supply you're partying on!"

"I told you you'd get compensated! And what do you mean,

you don't care who's occupying your moon? You don't think they meant to stop there, do you? Next thing you'd have 'em right here on your farm, eating up your supplies and parking all over your cornfields!"

"Looks to me like six o' one and three pairs of the other," the man muttered.

"If we let 'em get a foothold, they'll take over the whole cluster!" Sean continued. "It's not enough just to stand on the defensive. We've got to go after 'em!"

"Let's not overextend ourselves," Tolliver cautioned. "In fact, Sean, I'm wondering if it might not be a good idea to pull back to Blue Moon, and—"

"Pull back? Give up what we won on the field of battle? Not blooming likely!" Sean banged his mug on the table and looked fierce. "I've punched a message through to Jawbone to relay to the rest of the frontier worlds. As soon as the word gets around that we've got the Lobsters on the run, we'll get all the reinforcements we need! That's all I'm waiting for to launch a major offensive that will roll those Hatracks right out of the cluster like a wool carpet!"

"Maybe we ought to settle for just taking back what we started with," a sober-faced man said, rubbing his unshaven jaw. "Heck, I got ambition to—"

"That's just it!" Sean roared. "No ambition! Well, by hokey, I've got enough for the whole outfit! And I mean to see the Legion wipe the enemy off the map or get blasted into atoms trying!"

7

It was forty-eight hours when Harrumph tramped into the drafty hall in a blast of frosty air, stamping snow from his horny feet and shaking his grotesque head.

"It iss definite," he said. "For the past three hourss I've been in the comm sshack, monitoring fleet transmissionss. Hikop hass sstationed fully half hiss available forcess jusst out-ssysstem, interdicting any passage to or from Blacksstrap, while a large force gatherss off Blue Moon for a major assault!"

Sean, sitting at the table morosely cracking nuts with a

hammer, cursed as he banged a thumb, slammed the mallet aside.

"Where in the nine hells are those reinforcements?" he yelled. "I had a definite commitment from Saddlesore of three reconverted destroyers with full crew! Jawbone promised two thousand men! And Hardtack swore they were shipping me two Bolo WV tractors we could rig up as ground armor! And—"

"No use getting upset about it, Sean—" Tolliver started.

"Who's upset! And if this is supposed to be a military organization, it might be a good idea if you cowboys would say 'sir' once in a while!"

"Yes, sir!" Lisobel said smartly, coming into the room from the kitchen with a wide tray laden with soup bowls. "Dinner is served—sir! I hope you like brisket soup, sir. Because that's all there is, sir! The locals all say they want cash payment for supplies from now on . . . sir!"

"Arrhhh!" Sean clapped both hands to his head, planted his elbows on the table. "You can't run an army like a girl's school! I want a tight fighting force that can show those blasted Lobsters that a man will stand up and fight for what's his!"

Lisobel put the tray on the table and sat down beside him, contrite. She put her hands on his, smiled wanly.

"I'm sorry, Sean. Eat your soup. It's not bad. Your reinforcements will come along soon, and—"

"I'm kidding myself," Sean said flatly. "My last message must not have gotten through. We're cut off, overextended, undermanned, and outgunned! We've had it!"

"Shhh! Don't talk like that! You can send another message—"

"I've tried—six times, via the Bellerophon relay the last time. No soap. The Lobsters are jamming the whole band!" Sean rubbed a big, square hand across his orange-stubbled jaw. "Lucky for us, Hikop's got no way of knowing the shape we're in. One good slap would knock us over. We'd have to meet 'em with ball bats and pitchforks if they hit us now."

"If there's a spy in the outfit, he knows that, too." Cecil looked along the table.

"What do you mean, *if?*" Lou spoke up. "We *know* there's a spy here!" He hooked a thumb at Harrumph. "Even this Hatrack admits that much!"

Sean's face hardened. "I hate to think we've got a lousy renegade sitting right here at the table with us," he growled. "Whoever he is, when I catch him there won't be enough left of him to hang!"

"As long as he doesn't leave the planet, he can't do much harm," Tolliver put in reasonably. "I suggest we leave the spy-catching until later and concentrate on figuring out our next move."

"We're in a bad spot," Sean said. "And it's going to get worse before it gets better. Somehow, I've got to get word through to the rest of the Terry worlds, find out what's keeping 'em. And the only way to do that is..." He broke off and looked from Lou to Tolliver to Retief.

"Yes," Tolliver nodded, looking grave. "Somebody's got to go."

Lou snorted. "Don't look at me! I got through the Hatrack lines once, that's enough for me!"

Cecil wagged his head, looking doubtful. "I don't see how we'd get a man out through the whole blamed Hatrack Navy— and through the CDT surveillance net, too, Sean."

"As for penetrating Hikop's liness," Harrumph said, "there may be way. Give me few hourss with sstandard communicator sset, and I sshall code in analogss to hiss probe patternss. A lone boat sso equipped will be effectively invisible to at leasst his automatic detectorss!"

"See? What'd I tell you!" Sean beamed. "Old Rumpy's all right! By filbert, we may make it yet! Now..." He rubbed his hand across the side of his jaw. "We can use the postal skiff we picked up in town; it's got no armor, but it's small and fast." He looked at Lou. "You're out," he said flatly. "This is no job for a fellow whose nerves are shot—"

"What do you mean, shot—"

"And Cecil—well, you're a good man, but bare knuckles back of the barn is more your style than running a blockade on a delicate diplomatic mission...."

"But," Harrumph spoke up, "choice iss obviouss! Who elsse but redoubtable Bully Wesst! I happen to know that he hass already posed as diplomat on one occasion—with little ssuccess, as it happenss, through no fault of hiss own."

"Wha—" Lou started.

"Shut up." Sean cut him off short. "I've heard all the static I want to hear out of you, Lou!"

"You're nuts!" Lou stood and kicked back his chair. "You're all nuts!" He turned and stalked from the room.

Sean shook his head. "Lou's a funny fellow," he said, half-apologetically. "Seems like he's just turned kind of sour since the Hatracks raided Rawhide a few weeks back and blew a hundred-yard crater where his apple orchard used to be." He looked at Tolliver. "As it happens, I want Bully here as my tactical advisor. I was thinking about you, Lash. You've been around. You'll know how to talk to these Mule Kickers."

"It's really not in my line, this cloak-and-dagger business," Tolliver said diffidently. "But if it's what you want, Sean . . ."

"That's settled then," Sean slapped the table. "Well, boys, I guess that's about it. Harrumph, you get busy modifying that comm gear. Lash, you'll leave first thing in the morning—as soon as you get some rest." He caught Retief's eye as the others moved off.

"In a way I'd like to send you, Bully," he said to him in a low tone. "I've got a feeling you're a man I can count on. But I guess I need you worse here. Lash is a good man, but he hasn't got the drive I need in an Operations chief." He looked bleak. "If he doesn't get through, I guess the Terran Defense Legion will go under before it has a chance to show what it can do."

"I think Mr. Tolliver has hidden qualities," Retief said. "Don't worry, Sean. The message will get there—one way or another."

8

The room assigned to Retief was a low-ceilinged cubbyhole tucked far up under the eaves of the rambling old house, containing a bunk bed, a chair, and by way of wardrobe accommodations, a hook on the back of the door. After his guide had clumped away along the hall, Retief went to the small window, checked the latch. It opened easily. He swung the small casement out, looked down at a view of cobbled yard, silvery in the light of the newly risen moons, a stretch of lawn dotted with hastily erected tents. Beyond the stables, where the horned draft animals whined softly and shuffled their feet, lights gleamed in the equipment shed housing the courier boat, where Harrumph and the maintenance crew were still busy. To the left, along the wall, a stretch of rough masonry led to a tile downspout springing from the parapet of an intersecting wing fifteen feet away. In the other direction, the wall terminated at a corner a dozen yards distant. Below, light shone from a shuttered window one story down. As he watched, it winked out, leaving the house dark. Retief went to the door, listened, then opened it and glanced out.

At the far end, a husky youth with a power rifle slung over his shoulder leaned against the wall, yawning. He grinned and shuffled his feet.

"Uh, g'night, Bully—I mean Colonel," he said.

"Good night, Howie." Retief closed and bolted the door, flipped off the light, returned to the window. He swung a leg over the sill, and gripping convenient hand and toe holds in the rugged stonework, traversed the wall to the spout, shinnied up it, pulled himself over the parapet and onto the roof.

9

A heavy plank panel covered the access stairs leading down into a storage loft. Retief found his way down through the darkened passages into the empty dining hall, where red coals still glowed on the hearth, silhouetting a slim figure seated there.

"It's you, Mr. West," a slow feminine voice spoke softly. "Having trouble sleeping?"

"There does seem to be certain tension in the air, Miss Lisobel."

"Just Lisobel." Her long hair was tawny in the fireglow. "Don't you have any other first name than Bully?" she asked.

"I'd be honored if you'd call me Jame." Retief inclined his head, smiling faintly.

"For a mere soldier of fortune, you have rather courtly ways...Jame." The girl smiled almost sadly. "Not that I'm complaining."

"I suppose the headquarters of an illegal resistance movement is a pretty unromantic place for a young lady," Retief conceded.

"What? With all these dashing heroes and midnight plans

and breath-taking exploits?" She raised her eyebrows in mock amazement. "What could be more thrilling to a poor impressionable girl?"

"A peaceful home, maybe—and a large redheaded husband."

"I came along to help him," she said softly. "He's such a . . . a big boob in some ways—not that there's a man in the Legion who can stand up to him." Lisobel turned her haunting green eyes on Retief. "What sort of chance do we really have, Jame?"

"If the Haterakans don't move too fast—a good chance."

"And would those office boys back at CDT Headquarters really let them take Blue Moon—if they can?"

"Some of them would. It's all part of a larger plan, you see—"

"No! I don't see! These are our worlds! How can they just just sit there, and . . . and let some alien race take them away from us?"

"It's an old idea called Peace at Any Price. The theory is that by jollying the Haterakans along, in the end we'll all turn out to be good, good friends. But it would spoil things if in the meantime we shot at them."

"And the price is Blue Moon—and the rest of the frontier worlds of the cluster."

"Maybe not. Perhaps something will happen to change the CDT's mind for them."

"Something that you might have a hand in, Jame?" She looked away, shook her head. "No, I'm not prying. I just want to be sure that . . ." She stood, faced Retief. "He's a good man, Jame. An awfully good man. And he believes in what he's doing. You understand that, don't you?"

Retief nodded. For a moment Lisobel's eyes met his squarely. She leaned toward him, put a hand on his arm.

"Help him—all you can," she whispered.

"I will."

She tossed her head, swinging her tawny hair, smiled a brilliant smile. "And we'll both be more use tomorrow if we get some sleep now." She moved swiftly, kissed Retief lightly on the mouth.

"Good night, Jame. Somehow I feel better, knowing you're with us in this."

After she had gone, Retief stood for a few minutes, looking into the fire. Then he turned and crossed to a door, let himself out into a dark side passage.

9

Retief emerged via a side door into a walled garden plot. The night was icy cold; no breeze stirred. The air smelled of frost and fresh-turned soil and alien grasses.

Retief rounded the house, moving soundlessly in the powder snow, went along in the moon-shadow of celery-like trees to a small stone tool shed commanding a view along the path, across a fence and a line of shrubs toward the equipment shed. He stationed himself in the lee of the building, leaned against the wall, waiting.

A quarter of an hour passed in a silence broken only by the occasional clank of a tool or a raised voice from the shed, the whispering of the stiff fronds of the trees in the light breeze, the rustle and twitter of tiny night things aprowl. Then a light winked off in the shop, leaving a dim glow. Three men emerged, made their way across the yard toward the house. Retief caught a murmur of voices as they passed.

"...danged Lobster knows his stuff, I guess."

"Funny thing, him siding us. But I guess he's got his reasons."

"Ha! Catch *me* trusting that E.T. and heading into the Hatrack lines with nothing but a haywired IFF between me and a Lobster disruptor bomb..."

The door banged behind them. Another minute passed. A house door opened, closed softly. A tall figure emerged stealthily from the base plantings behind the manor, disappeared among the trees across the yard. Half a minute later a second dark form slipped from the shadows at the corner of the house, making via a roundabout route for the shed housing the courier boat.

Retief left his shelter, followed the line of trees, emerged between two utility huts at a point twenty feet from the shed entrance. Flat against the wall, he waited, listening. From inside the building came the sound of a soft electronic hum.

There was a sharp *click!* and the sound ceased. A moment later, the last shop lights went off.

"After you," a gruff voice said. Harrumph's ungainly figure appeared at the shed door. He stood aside, waited until the man with him had locked up, then turned to fall in beside him.

As he passed the dense growth of shrubbery, there was a sharp scrape of boots on hard ground. With a hiss, Harrumph leaped sideways, knocking his companion spinning as a muffled *whap!* sounded. A finger of actinic blue light scored a smoking gouge across the spot the alien had occupied. A man plunged from concealment beside the path, swung up a yard-long length of pipe, aiming a skull-crushing blow at Harrumph as he scrambled for footing. Retief stepped out behind the man, caught the bar just as it started its arc. The club-wielder yelped, yelped again as Retief delivered a solid kick to the seat of his plain gray coverall, sent him diving forward into the heavy growth from which he had erupted.

"Down!" Harrumph's hoarse voice snorted; Retief ducked as something whistled an inch over his head. A heavy body crashed through foliage just across the path. Retief spun to the alien.

"Run for it—that way!"

"And leave you to face the assassinss alone? Never!" Harrumph sprang into the underbush, from which the sound of heavy blows and muffled curses immediately issued. A moment later, a man tottered from among the wildly shaking leaves; Retief saw the glint of light along a gun barrel. He leaned sideways as the weapon flashed, stepped in and slammed a side-handed blow across the wrist holding it, caught a brief glimpse of a narrow, crooked-nosed face. With a curse, Lou stumbled back—and collided with a second man who stumbled, went down, slammed his head hard on the frozen path and lay still. Harrumph, reappearing at that moment, made a wild grab for Lou as the latter regained his balance and ran.

"Let him go," Retief called, but with a cry, Harrumph dashed after him in hot pursuit.

Retief took out a pocket flash, shone it on the face of the unconscious man at his feet. It was Tolliver, with a purple bruise already forming on the side of his jaw. Beyond him, the technician felled in the first moment of the fray groaned and rolled over.

Lights were winking on in the house now. Voices were shouting.

Retief whirled to the shed, tried the door, then caught up the bar dropped in the fray, jammed it in the chain lock and levered. The door burst inward. He jumped to the side of the scout boat, turned as a man tottered through the door behind him.

"Hey—don't touch that boat!" the battered technician blurted.

"Sorry," Retief said, and lanced a clean right across the man's jaw, caught him and eased him down at one side of the shed.

The boat's hatch stood open; Retief vaulted into the cockpit, slapped switches. As the whine of the power pack started up, he cycled the hatch shut, eased in the drive lever. The light boat slammed through the shed's rear wall, sending boards flying. Looking back, Retief caught a glimpse of startled faces staring up after him from pooled light in the cobbled yard. Then he nosed the little craft up in a screaming climb, barreling upward through light cloud cover until the scene was lost behind him.

2

Ten minutes later, Sean's voice, thin with distance, reached out to Retief as he hurtled away from Blue Moon, a misty orb now eight hundred miles astern.

"... I trusted you, West—and this is the way you pay me back! Tolliver's alive—and talking! He told me what he caught you at—you and that side-kick of yours! When I find that lobster-back I'll take the whole bill out of his hide!" His tone changed. "If there was any kind of excuse, Bully—I know you can't answer; you've got to hold communications silence till you're through Hatrack lines—but if I could figure any reason if you hadn't tried to brain Lash. I saw the crowbar you used on him. But the hell with it!" The snarl was back in his voice. "Why kid myself? You sold me out, West—and now you're running to your friends, with the only boat I could have gotten word out on. But I'll catch up with you some day—and when I do . . ."

Retief flipped the channel, picked up the spluttering of a Haterakan intership transmission. Far ahead, his long-range screens showed the close-set points of light that were the enemy blockaders. He held his course for another quarter hour before the gimmicked ID set *ding!*ed and flashed an amber light. A moment later the light winked off. Harrumph's adjustments, Retief noted with satisfaction, had successfully fielded the picket boats' probe beam.

Four more times in the next hour the modified IFF responded with the correct codes. The last challenger was a million-ton-plus carrier, a vast dark shape past which Retief's tiny boat hummed at visual contact range; but no weapon lanced out from the behemoth to impale the camouflaged blockage runner.

In the clear, Retief plugged in a course for Emporium, an uneventful sixteen-hour run. At the end of it, he dodged in past Atmospheric Control, ran a pair of revenue cutters a merry chase, landed, after losing them in a hair-raising course through rugged ravine country, in a dense stand of five-hundred-foot green-man trees on the reverse slope of a hill near a small city, domed against the dry, dusty heat of the arid torrid zone, on the opposite end of the continent from his first landing in the surf.

He hiked into town, took the tunnelcar to Discount, the planetary capital, stopped by a shop for a few small purchases, then checked in at the Commerce Hotel. After a needle-shower and autorub, he dressed in new garb dialed on the house servisystem, spent five minutes making certain arrangements in the closet, and went down to dinner.

3

As Retief sipped his second brandy, a fox-faced lad in a tight brown uniform came across the ankle-deep carpet, offered a gold tray with a small envelope with a pattern of pink jelly flowers.

"A message for you, Mr. Retief," he leered. "From a lady."

Retief flipped open the note, glanced at it.

"Where is this lady to be found?" he asked the bellhop.

"This way." The boy tipped his head toward the double doors at the far side of the busy dining room. "A swell looker," he added, and rolled his eyes.

Retief followed his guide out into a corridor decorated with slot machines, dope-stick and disease-prevention-device dispensers, and posters announcing a trade fair. Jittery music blared from closely spaced speakers concealed behind pots of artificial flowers.

"What's our destination?" he asked.

"The fountain, courtyard two, hundred and twelfth level," the messenger called carelessly over his shoulder. "Just follow me."

Retief overtook him in two strides, hooked a finger in the man's braided epaulet and spun him around.

"As I remember the plans of this hotel, the pile ends at ninety-five," he said.

"Here, leggo me jacket..." The bellhop broke off his expostulation as Retief took a notecase from an inside pocket of his midnight-blue evening blazer.

"How much did the other fellow pay you?" Retief inquired.

"Wha—what other, er, fellow, sir?" The youth blinked his eyes owlishly.

"The one who told you to keep me out of circulation for a while. I'd estimate it's about ten minutes' goose-chasing to the mythical hundred and fifth level; allowing ten minutes for a show of searching around for this mysterious lady and ten more to get back, that's plenty of time."

"Time for what, sir?" The boy rolled his eyes uneasily.

"Searching a room, for example." Retief extracted a twenty-credit note from the slim wallet. "This should top his offer. Forget the dry run. Let's go see *his* room."

"His room, sir?" The lad plucked the note from Retief's fingers and whisked it out of sight in a smooth motion. "Well, now, sir, that would be a bit of dirty pool—"

"Not half as dirty as my turning you in for picking my pocket."

"You mean that twenty was marked? Sir, you wouldn't!"

"Try me."

The bellboy opened his mouth, changed his mind, jerked a thumb over his shoulder. "Right, sir. His room. This way."

4

It was a first-class suite on ten level, adjacent to the nine-hole golf course. The steward keyed the door, glancing nervously along the soft-lit corridor.

"Just sing out if anyone comes along," Retief said.

Inside, he glanced over the standard hotel furnishings, the half-dozen drab suits in the closet, the snarled hairbrush and fussily rolled toothpaste tube in the bath. There was a locked briefcase on the bureau. He used a tiny instrument from an inside pocket to open it, glanced at the papers inside, snorted softly as he turned up a plastic-encased card.

Back in the corridor, he dismissed his guide, took the lift to his own level. In his suite, muffled sounds emanated from the direction of the closet. He pulled the door open. Inside, a small man in a nondescript gray executive coverall dangled awkwardly in a net suspended from the ceiling, his knees pushed up inside his ears, his arms trapped under him.

"I see you found the closet, all right," Retief said conversationally. "Cheap locks, for a flop as fancy as this one."

"I—I—it's a mistake," the small man choked. "Get me out of here!"

"What were you after?"

"I thought—I thought it was my lady-friend's room," the trapped intruder choked. "I . . . I was going to surprise her."

Retief glanced at his watch. "Uh-huh," he said. "Well, it's early yet. I'm in the mood for a leisurely *coq au vin*, preceded by a reasonable number of cocktails, of course. I should be back in three hours or so." He made as though to close the door on the hapless intruder.

"Wait! I—I'm not—that is, I *am*—I mean—you can't just leave me hanging here!"

"Why not? If I'd been busy visiting a friend on the hundred and fifth, say, I might not have come back at all."

"It was nothing like that!" the captive bleated. "Confound it, man, I'm a colleague of yours!"

Retief registered mild surprise. "Why, if it isn't Mr. Bloodblister, of Sector Headquarters, one of the CDT's top field men! For a minute I almost didn't recognize you."

"I should think not! I'm wearing five thousand credits' worth of the latest pseudoflesh make-up CDT Security could supply! Now cut me down at once, Retief!"

Retief aimed the ring on his left hand at the netted man; there was a tiny click as the camera recorded the spectacle.

"What's that for?" Bloodblister demanded.

"A little memento of our meeting," Retief said cheerfully as he released the net. "Neat, eh?" He invited the other's admiration of the trap. "I just rigged it for snoopers, of course. Hardly expected to net a DSO-2."

"You wouldn't *show* that picture to Ambassador Gumboil?" the nettee choked. "Or the Undersecretary!"

"Not unless it's necessary to scotch any exaggerated rumors that might get going among our mutual acquaintances."

Bloodblister tugged his rumpled clothing back in place, eyeing Retief sourly.

"I may as well come straight to the point, Retief," he said sharply. "I was dispatched out here specifically to find you. I'm to pass along new instructions to you—and to discover what explanation, if any, there might be for your failure to report progress in your assignment."

"Quite simple," Retief said. "There isn't any."

"No explanation?" Bloodblister raised a pale eyebrow.

"No progress," Retief corrected.

"See here." Bloodblister registered indignation. "You were sent out with instructions to get to the bottom of the rumors of Terran pirates and to secure Haterakan participation in PAUPER. Instead, you spent valuable weeks hopping from one world to another on a luxury liner, idling about the most elaborate bars the various provincial capitals boasted, and pursuing the acquaintance of a number of most unsavory characters before dropping from sight utterly   unless one excepts certain rumors too grotesque to mention!"

Retief nodded assent.

"Well, what have you to say for yourself?"

"It's been a very interesting cruise," Retief said. "Care for a drink, Mr. Bloodblister?"

"No, confound it! I'd like to be informed why you haven't filed your daily, semi-weekly, weekly, biweekly, and monthly reports, in sextuplicate, with attachments!"

"Too busy," Retief said.

"Too busy frittering away Corps funds?"

"That—and following up a few tenuous leads "

"Tenuous leads, indeed! Sector expects results, Mr. Retief, not alibis!" Bloodblister thrust out a thin lower lip. "If you've nothing further to add, in your defense " He reached for an inner pocket, brought out a long envelope bearing an embossed CDT seal, held it out.

"I have no choice but to transmit these orders from Sector, recalling you from your assignment."

"No posies this time," Retief noted, examining the missive.

"Jape if you will. But the fact is, Mr. Retief, the entire question of your future with the Corps is under close scrutiny at the moment!"

"Speaking of the future, I was planning to drop in at the Consulate to discuss that very subject."

"That won't be necessary." Bloodblister looked solemn. "At this moment a Special Investigating Committee is waiting to have a serious discussion with you regarding apparent malfeasance and gross dereliction of duty!"

5

A pregnant silence hung over the long table as Retief concluded his somewhat edited outline of the current state of affairs at Blackstrap and Blue Moon.

"Ahhh...Mr. Retief," a round-faced man with thick lenses, representing the Emporian Ministry of the Interior, broke the hush in a tone reminiscent of a mortician about to bring up the matter of payment. "Are we to, ah, understand that you, er, penetrated the inner councils of these, um, freebooters? That you, in fact, accompanied them on a foray, and personally witnessed the commission of atrocities against the persons of non-Terrestrials?"

"Almost right, Mr. Overdog," Retief corrected. "I spent a few days with the Terran Defense Legion; I saw them fight off an armed attack by a greatly superior force of the Haterakan Navy and thereafter re-occupy a small body the Haterakans had grabbed."

"Spare us these connotational subtleties," a purse-faced female DSO-1 with hair like a bleached sponge spoke up sharply. "Grabbed, indeed!"

Overdog placed his fingertips together carefully. "And now you say these, er, persons are plotting further, ah, violence—"

"Openly boasting of the intent to commit an aggressive act against an extra-Terrestrial people!" the lady member cut in.

"Please, Cirrhosa." Consul General Foulbrood, a spider-lean man in a drab gray midafternoon formal cutaway, raised a transparent hand, fixed a mouth like a torn pocket in a blood-chilling smile. "We must keep anything so subjective as personal emotion out of the discussion. Now, Mr. Retief: As I understand the situation, the main body of these ahem, irregulars, are for the moment licking their wounds at Blackstrap...." He turned, fingered a button, displaying a triagram of the frontier regions; Blackstrap and its two moons glowed a pale yellow. "While a second force waits at Blue Moon." The planet winked to a blue glow. "Meanwhile, the leader of the malcontents is soliciting collaboration in further unlawful acts of Jawbone"—a green light—"Mule Kick"—amber—"Saddlesore..." He enumerated the frontier worlds, arrayed in a loose crescent around Blue Moon.

"Aside from the loaded terminology, that's about it, Mr. Foulbrood," Retief agreed. "To which you might add the fact that a Haterakan fleet is disposed—"

"The CDT is not for the moment so concerned with justifiable responses of our neighbor races to the threat of violence," Foulbrood cut in, "as with the scope of the delinquency within our own ranks." He poked at another button; a scattering of tiny white lights appeared. "At present, CDT Peace Enforcement units are on station at the points you see designated here."

Retief nodded. "No wonder Braze's reinforcements haven't shown up."

"Yes," Foulbrood nodded complacently. "We've succeeded in pinching off the supply of new blood to the pirates by pinning down all would-be volunteers on their home worlds—"

"Tell me," Retief broke in. "What line will you take with the Haterakans when they move in to take over those same worlds?"

"It is hardly the place of the Corps to interfere with a natural readjustment of populations," the diplomat said smoothly.

"I see." Retief took out a dope-stick and puffed it alight, ignoring a chilling glance from Miss Latestitch. "It's all right if the Lobsters take over Terry-occupied worlds, but if the Terries fight back—"

"Terries! Lobsters!" Overdog's pale jowls quivered. "See here, there'll be no ruffian's cant tolerated at this Board! As for CDT policy, it's hardly the place of a discredited malfit of your stripe—"

"Calmly, Eucrustes," Foulbrood said blandly. "There'll be time later for a look at Mr. Retief's situation vis-à-vis the Corps. For now, sir"—he fixed a small, watery eye on Retief "suffice it to say that it is well within the scope of CDT capability to restrain any aggressive tendencies displayed by Terrans, but to seek to interfere with the sovereign acts of nonhuman governments is hardly in consonance with our Galactic Image!"

"Uh-huh. Feeding the cluster to the Haterakans is just one small chord in the background music Sector is wooing some bigger operator with. Too bad that wasn't mentioned in my pre-mission briefing. It might have made some difference in the way I handled my end of things."

"It's not use seeking to justify your failure by casting reflections on your superiors," Overdog snapped. "You're in serious trouble, sir." He rolled his eyes sideways at Foulbrood. As if on cue, the senior Board member raised a skeletal finger.

"However, all is not yet lost," he stated. "As you have stated, the ringleader of these dacoits has been isolated with only a few of his hard-core adherents in an essentially untenable position. Now, it remains only to snuff out this last pernicious pocket of decay, and we'll have a clean slate to show the Undersecretary." He showed his Yorick-like smile.

Overdog cleared his throat. "As it happens," he said, looking past Retief's shoulder, "a contingency plan has been prepared by

a Departmental Deep-Think Team for just such an eventuality."
He slipped a sheaf of papers from a flat briefcase on the table.

"It might even be, Mr. Retief," Foulbrood's blue-veined
eyelid quivered in a phantom wink, "that a role might be found
for you in the climactic ploy—provided you show a proper
appreciation of the gravity of the situation, that is."

"We can't allow these bandits to lounge at ease in their stronghold," Overdog put in quickly. "If the Haterakans, ah, make
contact with them there, innocent blood might be spilled."

"It will accordingly be necessary to coax them out into the
open," Fouldbrood pressed on. "Now, there is only one consideration which would tempt these troublemakers to abandon the
comparative security of a well-supplied base in the face of a
superior force of Haterakans: the hope of making contact with
the reinforcements they've been awaiting."

"They'll be messaged—in a most convincing fashion that a
concentration of volunteers is massing on a small body known
as Waterhole . . ." Foulbrood keyed his board, and a lone purple
light gleamed in the triagram, at a point half an A.U. in advance
of the frontier line. "Communications on the frontier being
somewhat difficult at the moment"—he twitched a corner of his
mouth—"the outlaws will have scant possibility of checking on
the information—information which they will be all too eager to
accept at face value."

"They'll embark their forces from Blackstrap," Overdog said.
"They will reach the rendezvous—and find nothing. Only a
bleak and airless orb."

"Not quite 'nothing' Eucrustes." Foulbrood quirked his
mouth. "A word to Grand Admiral Hikop should suffice to
ensure that these Bolsheviks will not be disappointed in their
desire to confront the Haterakans. There should be little
trouble: the rebels will be without reserves, poorly armed, and
vastly outnumbered."

"Very workmanlike." Retief blew smoke across the table,
watched Miss Latestitch bat at it with crimson-nailed hands.
"But why all the elaborations? Why not just station a couple of
P.E.'s off Blackstrap and pick them off as they come out? Or
even take them on the ground at Blackstrap?"

"A naïve question, sir," Foulbrood said drily. "These
so-called Legionnaires won't be taken without a struggle. I'd
hardly like to have my name associated with an armed encounter

between Corps Peace Enforcers and a band of Terrans albeit desperate criminals. The same holds true for a ground action. And innocent bystanders might be involved, to the detriment of my record. No, far better to lure the brutes into uninhabited space and deal with them there—"

"That might be a little rough on the Haterakans," Retief pointed out. "As you say, the Terrans will fight. How does that fit in with your tender feeling for our alien brothers?"

"The fate of a mere individual is of no interest to the Corps," Overdog snapped. "And as it happens, our exopsychologists say the Haterakans need a blood-sop to help drain off their aggressions—"

"Their justifiable resentments, don't you mean?" Miss Latestitch yapped.

"It's a sound scheme," Foulbrood said crisply. "The rotten apples are eliminated from the barrel, the Haterakans are properly appeased—and our hands are clean." He spread his hands, demonstrating their cleanliness.

"There's just one detail," Overdog said gruffly. "We'll beam the message through to the rebel chief, using a composite tape made up in our labs from transmissions we've intercepted from the frontier worlds during the last thirty-six hours—the same transmissions we've been jamming. He'll hear the voices of his contacts on the various worlds assuring him that he need only win through to Waterhole. However, there will of course be no way to, ah, make reply to any query he might have. And if we fail to respond, he may become suspicious. Therefore, it will be necessary for someone whom he knows to reassure him that all is well."

"He knows *you*, Mr. Retief," Foulbrood said softly. "He dispatched you on a mission of grave importance to his ambitions. What more natural than that you should bend every effort to contact him via CDT superbeam to give him the good news?"

"You expect me to talk to Sean, tell him to walk into this trap, is that it?" Retief said.

"Certainly." Overdog nodded.

"He trusts you, Mr. Retief," Foulbrood explained patiently, as to a dull-witted child. "It is precisely that fact which will make it possible for you to betray him."

6

In the gloom of the big transmission room in the Consulate cellars, the winking lights of the panels threw multicolored shadows across the alertly waiting faces of the assembled diplomats. From the monitors, the crackle of the faked messages came, weak with distance, almost lost in the jamming noise.

"...make it...," the voice of the planetary manager at Busted Axle whispered against the static. "...irregulars ...militia...arms. We've got...depot at Drygulch...on the way...rendezvous in twenty-nine hours from now...be there..."

"Nice job," Retief commented. "Your splice man is an artist."

"I don't mind telling you a considerable sum in Corps special funds went into this operation," Foulbrood said. "But I'm sure we can convince the auditors that we secured a bargain." He rubbed his hands together with a sound like a cicada shedding its skin.

"...Sean, best we can do," the chief of the Planetary Guard at Red Eye was saying now. "...we'll hit Waterhole in about thirty hours...ready to go...four thousand top-notch fighting men! We'll...these Lobsters what we can do! And..."

"Now, Mr. Retief, all you need do," Consul General Foulbrood cautioned, "is repeat the instructions to this pirate to move his force to Waterhole with all dispatch and assure him that a large force will await him there. You might do well to imply that you have, ah, hoodwinked some impressionable CDT official into looking the other way, in case he has doubts on that score; let him receive the impression that while the Corps can hardly espouse his cause openly, it fancies itself in the role of kindly behind-the-scenes sponsor of militant Terranism, that sort of thing, you know."

"I get the general idea," Retief said.

"...old, but by the Great Hairy...in top-notch shape," the unmistakable boom of Sourdough's Council chairman cut through the background hiss. "...be there...count on us, Sean! And...can't wait...see you soon..."

"That's it." Overdog spoke up as the recorded voices ceased. 'Now, Mr. Retief, it remains merely for you to cap the little performance with a stirring affirmation from an old comrade, eh? And we have the tiger caged!"

"I'm monitoring him now, sir." The communications technician looked up from his console. "A weak signal—about two by two—but you make it out." At a curt gesture from Overdog, he flipped a switch.

"...there on...awbone." Sean's voice, attenuated by half a light-year, broke from the speaker. "I read...confirm...thirty-five hours...O.K.?"

"Ah, he's cautious," Foulbrood showed teeth carved from mummy bone. "Well, we'll lay his doubts to rest, eh, Mr. Retief? And I think I can say"—he spoke in a tone of one imparting confidences—"that if this turns out well, I'll see my way clear to quash those charges against you, eh?" His eyelid nictated in a travesty of a comradely wink.

"Sure," Retief said. "I'll talk to him." He stepped past the broad-shouldered Marine guard standing by, fingering the strap of his rifle, leaned over the output panel.

"I'm holding my beam dead on him," the technician said. "Better make it fast. Punching through all that scrambled garbage and holding on target is like painting watch faces with a ten-foot brush!"

"CDT station Emporium to General Braze at Blackstrap," Retief said. "Sean, this is Bully West. You've just heard a transmission calling you to a rendezvous at Waterhole right?"

"West?" Sean's voice came back, distorted by the hyperlight beam that carried it. "...that...got the...talk to me? As...believe anything you'd say..."

"Listen to me, Sean," Retief said. "Listen carefully. Don't go! Repeat, ignore the message! Don't go to Waterhole! It's a trap!"

With a yell, Overdog leaped for the panel, slapped the master switch. Foulbrood yelped and barked a command. Retief turned. The power gun in the hands of the young Marine was aimed at the center of his chest. There was an astonished look on the guard's face, sweat on his upper lip—but the gun held firm.

"Now we see the full extent of your treachery!" Foulbrood hissed. "You're under arrest, Retief, for high crimes and gross breach of security! If it's the last thing I do, I'll see you shot for this like the mad dog you are!"

10

The cell to which Retief was conducted was a small commissary storeroom which had been hastily emptied of its stock of cased liquors, exotic food items and a wide variety of dope-stick brands.

"Being unaccustomed to treachers in our midst, we have no regular confinement facilities," Foulbrood said in a gravelly voice as a pair of perspiring workmen fitted a massive hasp to the greenwood door. "But I'm sure you'll find these accommodations secure enough. In view of the light-fingered tendencies of the locals, it was found expedient to construct the storage rooms with an eye to burglarproofing." The official seemed not to notice the looks shot him by the carpenters at this remark.

The hasp in place, Foulbrood produced an immense electrolock. At a gesture, the Marine guards shuffled their feet and rather sheepishly closed around Retief, loaded guns ready. He stepped inside the small room, and the door was slammed and bolted. Foulbrood's gaunt face peered in through the barred opening in the heavy panel.

"White you wait, you can perhaps solace yourself with the fact that your final treasonous act failed of its purpose," he said blandly. "By quick action, the technician was able to abort the circuit before the squirt pulser had completed its cycle. In fact, with a little dexterous cutting, I'm assured we were able to transmit an edited version of your ill-considered remarks which should serve nicely to close the noose."

"Nice work," Retief said. "By the way, how long do you estimate it will be before Admiral Hikop and his fleet arrive here on Emporium?"

"What's that? Emporium? Insofar as I know, no invitation has been extended to the Admiral to visit here."

"What's supposed to stop him? The path is wide open to the heart of the cluster—or will be, as soon as Braze has been eliminated."

"You're implying that the Haterakans will advance past Blue Moon?" Foulbrood pulled in his lower lip. "The Grand Admiral knows very well we're his friends; he wouldn't dream of doing anything so foolish..." A thoughtful look appeared on the diplomat's parchment face. "He wouldn't dare," he added in an undertone.

"Don't count on it, Mr. Consul General," Retief suggested gently.

"After all we've done for him? Good lord! If he *should* turn this way...!"

"You can stop him with a squadron of P.E.'s," Retief suggested reasonably. "Of course some people might wonder why it was necessary to fight a full-scale action in Terran space..."

Foulbrood emitted a stifled bleat. "A full-scale " He checked himself. "I see what you're doing, sir! Attempting to sow the seeds of suspicion! Save your efforts! In approximately thirty hours Haterakan jaws will snap on the bone we've tossed them, and that will be an end to the matter! As for you I doubt very much whether you'll be alive to see the triumph of Corps policy! Your case will be tried in the local courts—and the Emporians have a cluster-wide reputation for swift, businesslike justice!" He gave Retief a final glint of light from the glasses, turned and hurried away. The Marine guard looked after him, spat a gob of tobacco juice into a corner, and rolled an eye at Retief.

"I don't know what you done to get four-eyes mad at you, mister," he muttered, "but I'd as soon be locked in a phone booth with a pair of fire-lizards as have that old devil down on me!"

"Foulbrood's a valuable man," Retief said.

"Yeah," the Marine said. "A couple more like him and Hikop wouldn't need a navy."

2

Through the narrow eye-level window, Retief could see a stretch of dusty, walled courtyard, a wide arched gateway, a row of vendor's stalls under the trees lining an avenue of uneven shop fronts. Late sunshine reflected from gaudily colored signboards, sagging awnings, the motley garments of the hucksters, hawkers, stall-keepers, entrepreneurs, and customers who milled along the walkways. A clangor of voices, bells, the clash of goods being fingered by a hundred hands, the squeak of wheels, the clink of coins blended into a susurrus like restless waves on a rocky shore.

"Hey—you!" a raspy voice husked. A person in an elaborately pleated burnoose with an intricate pattern of food stains sidled close to the window, shot looks both ways, squatted down and made an elaborate show of lighting up a peculiarly vile-smelling dope-stick of Groaci manufacture. "New boy onna job, hey?" he whispered from one corner of his scruffy beard. "Howza bout angling a slice of the action my way, hah, chum?"

"Sure—why not?" Retief murmured in a conspiratorial tone.

"What I say is, why should them other slobs get all the gravy, you know what I mean? Pud knows I been in the game as long as anybody in the district!"

"You've sold me," Retief assured his new acquaintance. "When will you be ready at your end?"

"Boy oh boy, you really mean it? You're a fast operator, hah?" A grimy hand appeared and scratched the beard. Its owner hunched closer. "Look, I got a few irons in the fire at the moment, you know? Capital all tied up, see? I got to have a little time to set up a line of credit—"

"Deal's off," Retief said firmly.

"Have a heart!" the beard wailed. "Look, I'll get the cash! By the way, what kind of consignment you got?" A pair of beady eyes peered in past Retief, searching the gloom.

"The works," Retief said.

"Wow! You mean...?"

"All for you. But it's got to be a fast turnover, no later than tonight."

"Tonight? Holy chopsticks, Mac, how can I—"

"That's your problem; if you can't handle the proposition, I guess I'll just have to deal with the same old syndicate."

"O.K., O.K., I see your point. But look: don't make no sudden moves; I got a couple ideas, which if they pan out I can be here half an hour after sundown with my backers, right?"

"No later than that. By the way, you *do* know the delivery routine?"

"Sure—whatta ya think, I'm blind?"

"Better run over it once, just to be sure."

"Ah, fer—O.K. We time it between passes by the prowl car. You don't show no lights. The buyer flashes two greens and a pink from the third floor of the Discount Hotel across the way. Five minutes later the cart backs in by the delivery chute and you pass out half a load, collect, then deliver the other half. We split, stash, let the buttons go by, and run the same play past again. Now, I got to scram—"

"Just a minute. Where's the delivery chute?"

"Two yards left, fer the luvva Pud, Clyde! What kinda dummy you think I am, a cop?" He slithered and was gone.

"Two yards left, eh?" Retief murmured to himself. He checked the door; the Marine guard was leaning on the wall thirty feet along the passage, watching the stock girl's legs. Retief went back to the window, began an inch-by-inch search of the wall to the left of it.

3

It took him three-quarters of an hour to discover the fine crack between the lumpy oatmeal-colored plastic blocks, another half hour to deduce the precise angle and degree of pressure which caused it to pivot aside, revealing a narrow crawl space. Enough wan early evening light remained to show him the short tunnel opening into what appeared to be a coal chute, running at right angles to the partition.

Retief closed the opening, checked the guard again. He was still leaning against the wall, but the stock girl was with him now, looking up into his face with a rapt expression.

Beyond the window, the tone of the street noises had changed. The awnings were furled, the pushcarts jostling their way homeward through a thinning crowd. Lights had sprung up in cafés and small tables were being set out on the walks. From somewhere, a large population of overdressed ladies had appeared, unescorted, to take the chairs set out by the sidewalk eatery waiters. Behind the roofs, the sky was a deep twilight purple. In another fifteen minutes it would be dark.

There was a sound from the door. Retief turned.

"Uh, Mister." The guard was there, blinking into the darkness. "I just got some news. Looks like the Consul's pulled a few strings. They're not going to wait till tomorrow. Your trial starts in half an hour. Let's go!"

4

A key rattled in the door. It swung wide, revealing a second Marine, looking worried but ready, and a three-striper with a tight crooked-toothed grin.

"Out," the guard said. "We got orders to take you over to the Justice Building pronto."

"And from what Overdog said," the sergeant added in a snappy tone, "if you break for it on the way and we have to shoot you, that'll just save the taxpayers the price of a execution."

Flanked by the Marines, Retief walked along the passage, ascended the back stairs, stepped out into the courtyard where a closed van waited. A gaggle of bystanders gaped, open-mouthed, as the guards motioned him inside the bus. One of the Marines followed, while the others slammed the doors shut, clanged heavy locking bars into place.

A small window behind the driver opened, and the muzzle of a crater gun poked through. The car started and made a sharp swing, rumbling over uneven paving. The Marine sat stiffly, watching Retief.

"How much of this jazz is really true?" The youth said suddenly in a low voice. "What they're saying on the screens about some bunch of reactionaries trying to spark off a war out on the frontier."

"What's a reactionary?" Retief came back.

"Huh? Hell, I don't know."

"Where are you from, son?"

"Outpost. But—"

"Ever heard of the Terran Defense Legion?"

"Sure. That's our—but wait a minute! That's secret information! How'd—"

"I was there. Those are the reactionaries. They're walking into an ambush at a place called Waterhole."

"You mean—that's what . . . that's why . . ."

"No more talk back there!" a sharp voice barked from up front.

The car rolled on in silence for another five minutes. The young Marine fingered his gun and chewed the corners of his mouth.

Abruptly, there was a change in the engine sound, a sense of increased speed.

"Hey—it don't take this long to get to the Justice Building!" the Marine said suddenly. He turned to the wire-meshed peep-hole.

"Hey, Glotz! What's—"

The muzzle of the gun pivoted to point at the lad's chin. "Drop the popgun, sonny," a cheerful voice said. The other team has took over."

The gun hit the floor with a clatter. A moment later a larger panel slid back and a blunt-featured face grinned through.

"Hi, Bully," Jack Raskall said. "Looks like you made yourself plumb famous around these parts!"

5

"After Lou and me kicked loose from that Hatrack tub," Jack rattled on cheerfully as the hijacked vehicle rumbled along a moonlit country road, headed west, "we had a close brush with a Hatrack gunboat and split up. I took some damage and had to head for here. I been trying ever since to get myself a hop out

Blue Moon way. Then I seen you on the news, Bully; I knew you right away." He grinned from ear to ear.

"It was a slick idea, making out like you was some kind of CDT nancy. You sure fooled them bums—for a while, anyways. It's on all the channels, how you pulled some kind of flimflam on 'em and got yourself tossed in the tank. What the heck was you after, anyways, Bully?"

"Information, Jack. I think I've got all I need, now." Retief gave Raskall a capsule outline of his recent experiences with Sean's irregulars.

"Great news, Bully! You're the kind o' man we need in the Legion!" Jack took his eyes from the road to shoot him a look. "But it sounds like Sean's in some heavy trouble out there," he added.

"Hey," the disarmed sergeant seated between the two men growled. "Watch where you're going!" Jack casually swerved the speeding Black Maria back into his lane.

"Looks like this mug is particular how he gets killed," he grinned. "How about it, Bully? We're in the clear now. They haven't got the men to cover all the roads. I better pull off somewhere along here and we'll dump these slobs."

In a small clearing a quarter of a mile down a side track, Raskall motioned the captive noncom out, went around to the back, unlocked the heavy doors. The rear-end guard jumped down, gave Raskall a nervous look as the latter hefted a captured power gun.

"Hey," the sergeant said hoarsely. "You ain't gonna—I mean, cripes, you wouldn't...?" He swallowed hard. His freckles stood out starkly against his suddenly pale face.

"How about it, Bully?" Raskall cocked an eye at Retief. "Think maybe we better, uh...?"

Retief looked thoughtfully at the noncom. "If we let them go, they'll hotfoot it to the nearest phone and report in," he said.

"No, sir!" the sergeant burst out. Sweat was trickling down the side of his face. "Not a word! I won't say nothing! It ain't nothing to me if you fellers get away! Why, hell, I was just saying to Clem here, Hell, I says, it ain't nothing to me..." His voice trailed off.

"That right, Clem?" Retief looked at the younger man.

"He didn't say anything to me," the youth said sullenly. "He just now started spilling his guts."

"Why, you..."

"Shut up, Sarge," Raskall said easily and poked the gun muzzle into the other's chest.

"What about it, Clem?" Retief inquired. "Will you talk if we let you go?"

The lad looked at him. "I took an oath along with this suit I'm wearing," he said. "If you turn me loose, I've got a job to do."

"Hah!" Jack Raskall snorted. "I guess that don't give a man much choice—"

"Just a minute, Jack." Retief nodded toward the sergeant. "What about him, Clem?"

"Let him go, and he'll break a leg getting to a phone. He'll figure it's a short route to that fourth stripe."

"Got any suggestions?"

"Sure. Tie him up and leave him here. It'll do him good to spend a few hours out in the fresh country air."

"What about you?"

"Just keep pointing that gun at me." Clem's mouth twitched in an uncertain grin. "If you got a gun on me, I guess I'll have to go with you—and the way it sounds, that rebel general can use every man he can get out there on Waterhole."

6

For the next six hours Jack Raskall steered the captured car along bumpy back roads, unmolested. Just before dawn, a roadblock loomed ahead, a black and white barrier stark in the beam of a floodlight mounted atop a parked police flitter.

"Oh-oh." Raskall slowed. "Maybe we better take to the brush."

"Keep going," Retief said. "Clem, you talk to him. You'll know the right things to say."

"And if you get any big ideas, remember I still got a gun on my hip," Raskall muttered.

A uniformed Planetary Policeman stepped forward as the vehicle pulled to a stop. His light played over Raskall's face, took in his stolen police uniform, flicked to Clem, then to Retief.

"Whatza holdup, pal?" Raskall asked breezily. "Kinda early in the day to be manning a speed trap, ain't it?"

"Where you headed? Who's the plain john?"

"This here's Detective Captain Schultz." Clem nodded toward Retief.

The cop grunted, touched his cap bill with a finger. "You out of Discount?"

"Right." Raskall nodded emphatically.

"What's new on the jail spring that's got the bigwig's all stirred up?"

"How do we know, Sarge?" Jack shrugged expressively. "We been on the road all night."

"Yeah? What's the caper?"

Jack looked across at the newly christened Captain Schultz.

"Some people think he might have come this way," Retief said.

"Hah! Them doubledomes around headquarters, they ought to have their skulls candled! I ast ya, if *you* was to bust out of the can, would *you* hit the road for noplace, right out in the clear?"

"Well," Jack considered.

"You'd hole up," the cop confided. "Believe me, it was a inside job. This bum knew stuff them CDT johnnies didn't want spilled to the press, so it figures, how could they let it come to trial, right? So—the curtain! One'll get ya five that's the last we hear o' the bum!"

"Oh, I don't know," Raskall said, looking judicious. "Maybe the guy had a pal on the outside. Maybe he noodles a turnkey, grabs his threads, and cuts him out o' the cell right under their noses—"

"Ah, fer—you been seeing too many o' them midnight bone-splitters. Dresses up like a cop, hah? And rides the cop car right through the roadblocks, hey? You kidding?"

"Why not?" Jack demanded. "You think a guy couldn't do it? All he'd have to do is—"

"Ha! A phony cop yet! You think I couldn't spot a ringer the minute he sticks his head up? I got twenny years on the force—"

"How much you like to lay on that, Sarge?" Jack came back hotly. "Put you money where your mouth is!"

"Your mouth is going to put us all in the soup if you don't button it up—Sarge," Clem spoke up. "On account of being late," he added.

"Yeah." Jack opened his mouth, closed it firmly. "I guess you got a point there," he muttered.

"Get rolling, pal, before you start seeing little pink turkeys," the cop guffawed. He waved a hand and the barrier lifted. "Phony cops! Ha!"

"Wise guy," Jack muttered as he steered the car past the roadblock and gunned away down the road.

7

An hour later, Raskall guided the car down a bumpy, wooded slope, came to a halt at the base of a ten-yard-diameter green-man tree. The postal courier boat in which Retief had arrived on Emporium rested where he had left it on the carpet of fishing-rod-sized conifer needles.

The passengers climed down from the car, stretched their legs in the early morning sunlight filtering down through the towering stand of timber.

"You know, this ain't a bad world." Raskall drew a deep breath of forest air. "Plenty o' room to stretch out—and not enough cops to cramp a guy's style." He shook his head. "And them CDT bums want to give it away to a bunch o' Lobsters."

"We better not stand around too long admiring the view," Clem said. "We left a trail a mile wide. I admit the Planetary cops aren't much, but even they'll be catching on pretty soon."

Raskall looked the boat over critically. "Kind o' small, ain't it, Bully?"

"We can manage." the three men climbed into the cramped cockpit. "Better suit up," Retief suggested, and handed out packaged emergency suits from the locker under the seat.

"Hey, there's some kind of cargo back here," Clem announced from his position in the storage compartment behind the pilot's chair. He hauled out a heavy gray mail sack marked DIPLOMATIC and sealed with the CDT seal. "Feels like books," he said, hefting it.

"Looky here," Raskall blurted, fingering the address tag. "This here's consigned to the Hatrack world!"

Retief pressed the seal with the proper code, reached in the bag and drew out a fat volume profusely illustrated with glossy tridographs in full color.

"It's harmless," he said. "Just an idea a gentleman named

Magnan had for uplifting the Haterakan masses."

"O.K. if we toss 'em out?" Clem inquired. "There's a pile of them back here."

"Let 'em lay," Jack Raskall grunted. "Out on Waterhole we can use 'em to start fires with."

"It won't be a picnic out there," Retief said. "If anybody doesn't want to go, this is their last chance to opt out."

"I'm with you," Clem said. "You're still holding a gun on me, you know."

"Let's lift, Bully," Jack said. "Sean's going to be needing us bad by the time we get there."

11

A lone Planetary Patrol craft challenged and gave brief chase as the courier boat hurtled outward from Emporium, but was swiftly outdistanced and left astern. Ten hours later, a pair of Haterakan warships, cruising deep in Terran space, hailed the tiny boat. Its automatic IFF gear chattered a brief reply. Unsatisfied, one of the vessels altered course, transmitting a verbal command in harsh Haterakan.

Retief checked his fuel gauges, fed figures to the course computer.

"Let's see how bad he wants us," he said, and reset the panel for emergency maximum drive. The boat leaped away at 2.7 G's of acceleration. For half an hour the big ship hung on; then it broke off, veered away to return to course.

"Looks like he had important business elsewhere," Jack chortled.

"It's not just Blue Moon and Waterhole the Admiral's interested in." Retief pointed to the navtank. Around the glowing images of every Terran-held planet within half a dozen

133

A.U.'s faint traces indicated the convergence of heavy units of the Haterakan Navy.

"Looks like old Hikop's getting in position for a full-scale takeover!" Jack blurted. "Well, there's one consolation: that won't leave him much to hit Waterhole with."

"How much will he need?" Clem inquired, frowning. "From what you say, the rebel general can't have more than a couple hundred men with him."

"We'll find out soon," Retief said. "I just picked up Waterhole on the forward screens, forty-one minutes dead ahead." He cut all power, neutralized all radiation sources, and erected the radar screens. "Let's see how close we can get before they spot us."

2

"Boy," Jack Raskall muttered half an hour later, staring into the screens alight with the glowing red blips that indicated Haterakan gunboats. "The Lobsters are in around that rock like sugar-flies on a jelly flower."

"All small stuff," Retief said. "I have an idea Hikop's planning on doing a little face-saving by cleaning up Waterhole with the minimum of fuss and bother."

"Sean's only got nine boats," Jack mourned. "Hikop must have fifty!"

"Hey!" Clem looked up from the shielded communicator on which he had been microbeaming the Legion's recognition code. "I got a beep on locus 476..." He twirled vernier knobs on the screen on which Waterhole was now a gleaming point against the blazing backdrop of the cluster. "Yeah! I'm reading their ID echo, Mr. West! They're down there!"

"Anyway, they're still alive," Jack muttered. "Which is more than we'll maybe be in a few minutes."

The rock known as Waterhole swelled to an irregular disk, as the tiny courier craft swept inward, ignored so far by the swarming gunboats ahead. Then, abruptly, the IFF chattered in response to a probing beam from an enemy vessel.

"Here it comes," Jack said between clenched teeth. "They got us on visual now." Again the IFF clucked its automated response. As it clicked off, a Haterakan voice burst from the speaker, barking an obvious challenge.

"Hold tight, everybody," Retief said, and switched on power, threw the boat into a spine-wrenching evasive pattern. At once, bright points of light blossomed on the screens as the Haterakan's relay-triggered batteries opened fire. The DV screen flashed white and dimmed as a warhead burst nearby, its overloaded protective circuitry buzzing indignantly.

"It's...hell...not being...able...to shoot back...," Raskall gasped out as the boat twisted, bucked, flipped end-for-end, veering around, under, past and through the barrage hurled at it from a dozen units of the Haterakan force, whose missiles, rigidly tracking along pre-computed courses, detonated harmlessly off-target, defeated by the unpredictable dartings of the minuscule craft.

"We're through the outer line," Raskall blurted as a final pair of interceptors dwindled astern. "If the danged Lobsters'd thrown out a random pattern, they'd of nailed us!"

"Uh-huh," Retief said. "Here come the inner defenses!" An enemy cutter rushed toward the intruder, firing white bursts from its braking jets as it strove to match courses. Swiftly, it grew, sliding across the screen. At the last moment, it fired a salvo which rushed harmlessly past, prevented from detonating by safety devices aborting a burst within the parent vessel's vulnerability radius.

Another Haterakan approached, this one a small pursuit ship. Light crackled from its prow as it fired a fixed-mount power cannon from maximum range. Retief threw the boat aside from the lancing beam, rolled it on its back, dropped toward the rugged surface now only miles below. The attacker hurtled past, swerved in a screaming U to follow its quarry in a headlong dive. On the forward DV screen, the rocky peaks below—stark black and white in the unfiltered glare of the star—rushed upward with breath-stopping speed. At the last possible instant, Retief flattened the racing craft, shot past a row of dagger-points upthrust from a lava flat, and across the terminator toward inky blackness ahead.

"You're too low!" Raskall shouted. Retief shook his head, held the fleeting vessel on a flat-out course across the level plain blurring beneath him. Ahead, a dimly seen shape of rock swept closer, closer—

Retief hauled back on the controls, lifted the boat in a

vertical climb past the rock face rising up, up—

From below and behind, white light blossomed, turned ruddy, faded. A dull shock shook the speeding boat.

"N-neat maneuvering B-Bully," Raskall choked. "You lost him."

"Some splash," Clem said. "Better steer oh-nine-eight now, Mr. West. My last reading says we're close!"

"There!" Jack pointed ahead, where brief, incessant flashes lit the close horizon. "A barrel to a bar rag that's Sean and the boys—on the getting end of everything the Lobsters can throw at them!"

"Not only them," Clem said in a strained tone. "They're ranging us, too!"

The bright trajectories of tracers were arcing in toward the tiny boat's course now; a vivid burst etched faces starkly in the crowded cockpit. The boat rocked and shuddered. At the controls, Retief swerved the low-winging craft, aimed it toward the center of the action ahead. At an altitude of less than a hundred meters the boat hurtled over a small crater, where the massed fire of the enemy converged like sparkling fire hoses on the tiny, flickering dome of a force bubble.

"They're pinned down like a butterfly collection," Jack groaned. "The boat's screens are holding so far, but they can't last long under that!"

"And there's no way for us to get inside—" Clem's voice was drowned in the clangor of a thousand Chinese gongs being slammed by a thousand steel mallets. The boat leaped as if kicked by a mighty boot. Retief fought the controls, righted the tumbling boat, slammed down the red EMERGENCY RETRO lever. The boat surged, sank sickeningly. With a dizzying slam, the tiny cabin spun, jumped, struck and bounced, touched down again, skidding amid a crashing roar of ripping metal and splintering rock, came to a halt half on its side in a leisurely clatter of slowly falling debris.

"We're...down!" Clem gasped out.

"Yeah—but did we live through it?" Jack coughed.

Retief pulled himself free of a tangle of wiring which had burst from behind the dislodged panel, tripped the escape hatch level, pulled himself up and out, looked around at a rocky landscape lit by a blaze of stars intermittently brightened by the wink and stutter of guns firing near at hand.

"It's plumb unhealthy around here," Jack called as he jumped down. "Let's head for cover!"

Retief led the way to a dark cleft in the rising rock ahead, Jack and Clem trailing.

"Hold it!" Retief said quietly, and waved the others back.

"From fifty feet away, a beam of light flicked out, speared him.

"As I susspected," a familiar voice croaked. "Bully Wesst! I told you hiss style of landing sspacecraft iss unmisstakable!"

3

The Haterakan picked his way across the broken ground, a tall, ungainly creature in an oversized vac helmet, still wearing his tattered tunic, hanging open over chipped chest paint, a bedraggled but still jaunty caricature of the once splendidly caparisoned officer.

"I advissed the General that you would return in fullness of time, but alass—he wass ssskeptical." The alien's voice grated in Retief's earset like boulders stirring on a river bottom.

"Sorry about leaving without an explanation," Retief said. "I'm glad to see you made peace with Sean."

Harrumph laughed hollowly. "Hiss termss were irressisstible," he croaked, and held up his arms—both pairs. Heavy manacles linked his wrists. "He cannot bear to be parted from me, it sseemss. He insisted that I come along on this mad venture—"

"Where is he?"

"If the sslave iss here, can the masster be far behind?" Harrumph tilted his head rearward; a massive space-suited figure clumped forward from between towering rocks, took up a stance with a cradled blast rifle aimed at Retief's chest.

"You got some nerve, showing your face here, West," Sean growled. "You can say your prayers now, before I blast you off this rock!"

"Hey—just a minute, Sean!" Jack Raskall came hastily forward. "You're going off half-cocked! Bully's here to help out!"

Sean emitted a surprised grunt. "Jack Raskall! What are you doing keeping company with this sharper?"

"Wait a minute, Sean! This is Bully West, my old pal from

back home! Heck, you remember Bully!"

"From—where'd you say?" Sean's voice was sharp.

"Home! Outpost! Him and me grew up together in Broken Bone—but heck, Sean—you know that well's I do!"

"Do I?" Sean turned on Retief. "That does it," he said flatly. "Broken Bone is my home town, too. Lived there all my life. And I never laid eyes on this fourflusher till last week!"

4

"It must be a case o' that amnesia like you hear about," Jack said stubbornly. "Bully's the oldest buddy I got—"

"Somebody's been tinkering with your head, Jack," Sean cut him off. "This slicker's fooled you—but he's not fooling me."

"Sean—don't you trust me?" Jack almost screeched.

A nearby burst rocked the ground, sent shrapnel hurtling in ghostly silence past the heads of the group.

"I notice there's a fight going on," Retief said. "Maybe it would be better to handle that first and defer the explanations until later."

"There'll be no 'later' for you, you back-stabbing son of a—"

"Back-sstabbing?" Harrumph spoke up. "He merely made use of your boat for little trip—and now he hass returned it!"

"Stand back, Jack," Sean said coldly, and raised the gun. "I'll get this over with right now!"

"Sean—you can't do it!" Jack yelled.

"He won't get the chance," a new voice spoke from behind Retief. Clem stepped forward, his heavy police model power gun gripped in his fist. "You're on the wrong tack, General. We came here to help—all of us. Mr. West told me all about the dirty deal you got. He's on your side—"

"You—drop the weapon!" another voice commanded from behind Sean.

For a moment there was absolute silence. Clem covered Sean; Sean's weapon was aimed halfway between Retief and the former policeman.

"Better do as he says, Clem," Retief called.

With a muttered curse, Clem tossed down the gun. At once, a suited figure stepped forward from the shadows behind Sean.

"You won't have to soil your hands with this traitor, Sean,"

Lash Tolliver said. "I'll attend to him." He raised his crater rifle quickly, threw off the safety There was a wink of vivid blue light, the harsh buzz of a power gun. Tolliver took a step forward, dropped the rifle, leaned, fell slowly forward on his face. With a yell, Sean spun, bringing his gun around; another wink of blue, and the blaster flew from his hand.

"Sorry, Sean," Lou said, coming forward. "About messing up your gun, I mean, not that rat." He jerked his head toward the body on the ground. "This fellow West or whatever his name is— he's not the traitor. Tolliver is."

5

Five minutes later, inside the ringwall, Sean looked at Lou questioningly.

"How did you find him out?"

"I caught him when he tried to brain this Lobster of ours back at Blackstrap. We rassled a little in the dark, and this fell out of his pocket." Lou showed a small cylinder. "Took me a few days to dope it out. It's a Hatrack code book with a message all coded, ready to send. He meant to turn us over to this Hikop, lock, stock, and likker barrel."

"You might have sspoken up ssooner," Harrumph suggested. "But perhapss you were not aware I disslike being chained like wild beasst."

"I wasn't dead sure, until West came back," Lou said. "When I came up just now and saw Tolliver ready to gun him down well, it was too late to do anything but what I did." He looked at Retief awkwardly. "I still don't know just what your game is, mister. But anybody that'd come in here now, through what you had to come through, has got to be on our side."

"There are flawss in your reassoning," Harrumph murmured. "But who am I to point them out?"

"You came back here to help, did you?" Sean said bitterly. "But" his expression brightened—"but hell! You went to get word to my reinforcements! Why else did you take the boat! You must have been tipped to what Tolliver was up to, and instead of trying to convince me, you just made the run yourself, right? Well, where are they, Bully? When do they get here? How many "

"Sorry, Sean," Retief said. "No reinforcements."

"You mean—they all let me down?" Sean sounded incredulous.

"They tried to get here. They ran into interference—not from the Haterakans."

Sean nodded slowly. "So that's it," he said thickly. "I should have figured . . ."

"That leaves it up to us," Jack said. "I hear you've got nine boats and about two hundred men and plenty of guns and ammunition—"

Sean laughed, a harsh bark. "I wish I did, Jack! With two hundred men, I'd hold this rock forever!"

"What you mean, Sean?" Jack sounded puzzled. "We thought—"

"You thought wrong," Sean said in a bitter tone. "Look around! I've got what's left of one boat and twenty-two men.

6

We were half an A.U. out when the Peace Enforcer jumped us," Sean said. "At the first hail, I gave the order to scatter. They were fast, but not quite fast enough. My boat was the only one got clear."

"Cripes! You shoulda turned back for Blue Moon—" Jack started.

"I had a rendezvous to make at Waterhole," Sean said harshly.

"Well, you made it," Jack said. "Must o' been kind of a bad scene when all you found here was Lobsters."

"I got here first—just barely. I had time to pick a defensive position and set up my perimeter line inside the boat's repellor field. Half an hour later, they hit us. That was three hours ago. We've been hugging rock ever since."

"Lucky it's all light stuff," Jack said. "The Lobsters could blow this rock into hot gas if they felt like it."

"They're trying to buy us cheap," Sean said. "But we'll keep the price up—as long as our ammo lasts."

Standing beside the grounded boat which marked the center of the embattled Terran position, Sean studied the flickering aurora surrounding the small crater, the ringwall of which protected his tiny detachment from direct ground fire.

"You got here during a lull, Bully," he said. "I guess maybe Hikop's discovered he can't poke a hole in a meteor screen with firecrackers. He'll be trying something else pretty quick now."

"I'd just as soon he'd go ahead and get it over with," Lou said. "It's getting to me, sitting here with my fingers in my ears, watching the boomers and sizzlers bounce off that pint-sized shield. They look like they're dropping right into our laps."

"It won't hold long," another man said. "I checked her power reading just now. We've got maybe another hour."

Sean looked at Retief. "What about it, Bully? Any ideas?"

"How many troops does Hikop have out there?" Retief asked.

"My best estimate is two thousand," Sean said. "With tracked armor, hand weapons, some field artillery, all non-nuclear so far."

Retief nodded. "He's playing a touchy game; he can only go so far without making the CDT take official notice."

"All he has to do is sit tight and keep enough pressure on us to drain our power cells," Lou said. "Then—*ff-fftttt!*"

"Still—we don't have to sit here at ground zero and wait," Retief said.

"What do you mean, Bully?" Sean demanded.

"We're in an untenable position, from the defensive standpoint," Retief said. "So our next move is obvious."

"Yeah." Sean grinned fiercely. "I figured you'd say that: attack!"

"Sounds good," Lou grunted. "I'd like to lob something into those babies—but how do we start?"

"I suggest we start by moving to a new position," Retief said. "And then we can look over our arsenal and see what we can throw back at them."

"It's kind of a risky idea," Sean said thoughtfully. "But the Lobsters won't figure us to crawl out from under our umbrella as long as it's keeping the rain off. We can slip out along the gully and leave 'em shelling an empty crater." He smacked his fist into his palm. "O.K.; it's better'n sitting here and doing nothing. Pass the word, Lou: Pack up and be ready to pull out in five minutes!"

7

Half a mile from the abandoned crater, the party emerged from the shelter of the fissure along which they had retired, sheltered from the barrage, and looked back at the abandoned stronghold.

"Looks kind o' pretty from here," Jack Raskall said. "Like a big Discovery Day fireworks show back on Outpost."

"Yeah. Well, it'll look prettier than that in a few minutes, if this scheme works out. Lou, set up your mortars along that ridge and zero 'em in on the crater. Harry, you take ten men and get up that rock spine; but don't fire a round until the mortars let go!" Tersely, Sean gave his orders to his pitifully small force.

"Now, I guess we just wait," he said.

"Not for long." Jack shook his head. "That bubble's shrinking fast."

"Once power level dropss below metering valve minimum, end iss closse," Harrumph volunteered. "Only secondss now..."

Abruptly, the barrier, visible only as an intangible surface against which the Haterakan beams played fruitlessly, dwindled inward upon itself, flickered briefly with a play of waning color, and was gone. At once, the arcing traceries of the Haterakan fire ceased. The abandoned boat, standing tall and slim against the starry sky, was outlined by a beam of blue-white radiance, then another and another. The searchlights played across the ground, revealing broken rock, a few scattered candy-bar and dope-stick wrappers, some empty ammo boxes.

Retief's earset crackled as an outside transmitter, broadcast an all-wave carrier. He switched off the interference filter.

"Terranss!" a Haterakan voice rasped. "Ssurrender at once or be annihilated! You have sixty ssecondss! Thiss iss your ssole and final warning!"

"Hold your fire," Sean rapped as a man shifted position nervously. A minute passed in utter silence. There was a sudden boiling up of dust from around the periphery of the crater. Starlight glinted on armored figures, rising from concealment, advancing from all sides on the supposed Terran position. They mounted the low ringwall, scrambled over boulders, slid down the inner slope, while behind them, tracked vehicles trundled forward, guns depressed for point-blank fire.

"Harry—pick off the foot soldiers," Sean commanded. "Lou—there's ten cars in sight; one target per mortar. Be sure each gunner knows which one's his!"

"If you ssee taller-than-average chap with gold cranial sspines—sspare him," Harrumph croaked. "Honor of Avunculate demands I deal perssonally with Grand Admiral Hikop."

Under the lights, the Haterakan troops were spreading out over the crater floor, poking into crannies, peering behind boulders, looking for Terrans. The cars, picking their way through the occasional breaches in the encircling wall, were topping the rise now, grinding rock to powder under their treads as they trundled downward, their headlights cutting white swaths through the dust.

"O.K., Sean," Lou whispered hoarsely. "On target and primed!"

"You ready, Harry?" Sean called.

"Never readier," Harry grunted.

"Then FIRE! And at the word, a crash of thunder shook the rocks; ten mortars hurled their fractional kiloton warheads up and over to detonate in blinding flashes among the enemy armor, while Harry's gunners poured streams of fire among the scattering troops.

"I see two tanks on their sides!" Sean shouted. "Three . . . four . . . five with blown treads or on fire! Lou! Pour another salvo into the two that are still moving!"

"There's more Lobsters coming over the rise!" Harry called.

"Pin 'em down! Lou—" The mortars crashed again; a surviving car leaped, spun. The other rocked, emitting smoke from its upper turret. Its hatch flew open, and three Haterakans leaped down, dived for cover as Harry's independent hand-blaster fire sizzled after them.

"One more time!" Sean called. The mortars boomed out a third ragged volley—and then on command, the men were up, falling back behind the next ridge.

"Come on, Bully!" Sean slid down from the perch from which he and Retief had monitored the action.

"Nine cars out of action," Retief reported as he joined him. "That ought to teach Hikop a little caution."

"And if he gets cautious enough, maybe we'll take him yet." Sean showed a fierce grin through his dusty faceplate.

"At least it will help keep us alive a little longer," Retief said. "Now let's hit him again before he has time to get over being surprised and starts getting mad."

8

Ten minutes later, from a new position, Retief, Sean, Lou, Jack, Harrumph, and the twenty-one men of the command watched as concentrated fire swept the ridge they had vacated minutes earlier.

"Old Hikop's thorough," Sean said. "But his reaction time is slow."

Lou lowered the electronic binoculars through which he had been observing the activity in the overrun crater.

"Something going on around the boat," he said. "Maybe he's getting ready to lift her off, Sean." He smiled a wolf smile at the redhead, who grinned silently back.

Moments later, with a rumble the men felt through the rock, the tall ship stirred; light flared at her stern. Gracefully she lifted on a column of translucent blue fire.

"Duck!" Sean barked—and followed his own advice as a blinding white fireball replaced the ascending vessel, bathing the landscape in its stark glare. A Haterakan car perched on the crater rim was outlined in silver brilliance for an instant before it toppled over out of sight; running soldiers, caught near the exploding ship, were hurled away like tenpins before a rolling dust cloud obscured the view.

"I booby-trapped her," Sean said in tones of satisfaction. "And we caught a few boobies that time."

Something large and dark flashed across the sky, light flickering from ports along its belly. Rock splintered and burst nearby; a man shouted, fell to the ground, swearing, gripping his leg. A second low-level bomber howled past, scattering its cargo wide to the left. A third boomed into view, dead on target.

"Scatter!" Sean yelled, and the men dived for the meager shelter of rock slabs as a stick of H.E.'s gouted dust across the ridge.

"Bully! You all right? Lou! Harry!" Sean's voice racketed in Retief's earset.

"A little noise, that's all," Lou grunted a reply. Other men reported in on the command linkage.

"We've got a casualty over here, Sean," Retief reported. "It's Kelly. A broken leg."

At Sean's instruction, the little band regrouped, carrying the wounded with them, gathered in a hollow almost over the curve of the tiny world's horizon from the Haterakan concentration.

"We've got just one advantage," Sean said hoarsely. "They don't know where we are, and we're hard to spot. They're throwing out enough stuff to flatten a city, but most of it's going wide of the mark."

"We've lost three wounded, out of action," Lou said. "And with no medic a couple of 'em'll be dead by dinner time. Yeah, maybe we knocked out a hundred Lobsters—but I still don't like the odds."

"Then let's shave 'em a little," Sean grunted. "Set up and get ready to blast any ground party Hikop sends out."

"I lost a mortar, you know," Lou said. "Kelly's."

"Hey, here they come!" Harry pointed. A loose skirmish line of Haterakans was advancing from three sides on the last position evacuated by the Terrans.

"Mortar fire's no good against deployed infantry," Lou barked.

"Harry, wait until they're a hundred feet clear of their cover," Sean directed. "Then let 'em have it!"

Retief, using Lou's binoculars, scanned the airless expanse of rock stretching before the Terran position. Two hundred yards distant, the Haterakans closed in on their empty objective, starlight glinting on their armor, here and there the gaudy plumes and spines and epaulettes of an officer lending a note of color to the grim scene.

Retief scaled a low mount, swept the offside areas. Nothing stirred there. To the rear, a close ridge barred his vision.

To the left, halfway to the ridge, a lone spire of rock loomed. He slid down from his perch, in great, low gravity bounds crossed to it. Behind him, a sudden winking of light denoted that the Terrans had opened fire. Retief reached the finger of rock, jumped, caught a rock, jumped, caught a handhold, pulled himself up to a position from which he had a clear view over the ridge. In the darkness there, something moved....

"Sean!" Retief called the Legion commander via headset. "Drop everything and run for it! Half the Haterak Navy will take you in the rear in about thirty seconds!"

9

Lying flat on a narrow ledge halfway up the rockspire, Retief took aim at the narrow defile through which the lead element of the flankers was about to emerge. As the blunt prow of the first vehicle appeared, running without lights, he fired a narrow-beam blast at the rock above it. A massive slab slid down, crunched heavily across the armored car's turret. Sparks flew and dust boiled up as the tracks churned in a vain attempt to plow clear of the multi-ton obstruction. Behind the car, others halted, while foot troops ran forward, scrambling up and over the barrier—to meet the pin-point fire of Harry's gunners, shooting as they ran, while the Haterakans poured in a return fire.

Retief dropped down in the shelter of the spire. Keeping low, he made his way across the open stretch, reached the tumbled rock where the main body of the Terrans had taken refuge. The survivors numbered fourteen men—four of them wounded— and one Haterakan, with three mortars and half a dozen rounds of ammunition.

"I knew our luck couldn't last," Lou said darkly.

"We're alive, aren't we?" Sean shot back. "And Bully here saved our bacon for us—most of it."

"I think," Harrumph volunteered, "that Hikop might still entertain ssurrender offer, in sspite of hiss earlier threat—"

"Surrender, hell!" Sean grated. "I didn't come here to give up!"

"Excellent," Harrumph nodded. "With luck, I'll sstill get clear sshot at Hikop before we die."

"We've hurt 'em," Sean said. "By the nine devils, they know they've been in a fight! And they'll be in some more before they root us out of this spot!"

"We can shelter down in the crannies amongst the rocks if they try to soften us up with artillery," Harry said. "Then pop up and blast 'em when they come in on foot to clean up."

"Which won't be long now," Lou said. "They know how many of us there are now; they got a good look when they flushed us."

"My ssole hope," Harrumph stated, "iss that the sscoundrel, Hikop, will not be sso lacking in zeal as to fail to join in the assault." He patted his power rifle. "I sshould prefer to throttle him manually, but under circumstances I am prepared to ssettle for bullet between hiss eyess."

"Oh-oh," Harry said. "Looks like this is it, fellers . . ." Across the rugged stretch of terrain, armored figures were in motion, moving up in quick dashes from one shelter to next, forming up an assault line that stretched around in a wide curve all across the front.

"Well, boys," Sean said solemnly. "I never meant to lead you into a fix like this—but now we're here, I know I can count on every man of you to do his duty to the last. Not much glory in it, I guess—but maybe what happens here will wake some people up to what's going on. Maybe we'll show the Lobsters—and some Terries, too—that a man stands up for what's his."

Below, the movement had ceased. Half a mile distant, the wreckage of the ship still burned fiercely, casting a yellow light on peaks and edges of rock, pooling the plain in shadow.

"What . . . what you reckon they're waiting for, General?" a voice that quavered a trifle inquired.

"That's Sean, Len," Braze said gruffly. "We're in this together, man to man. As for what they're doing—they're trying to wear our nerves down a little, would be my guess."

The boy unlimbered a bulky object slung over his shoulder. "How . . . how about a song . . . Sean?" he said, holding his voice steady.

"You mean you still got that git-fiddle, after all we been through?" Harry demanded. "Glory be, boy! Good for you! How about 'That Little Old Rock Called Home'*?"

"Yeah!" other voices chimed in. "That's the spirit, boys!"

Beside Retief, Harrumph hastily flipped down a toggle at the side of his helmet to switch his earset from the command frequency. Catching Retief's eye on him, he leaned to touch helmets.

---

*Copyright A.D. 2939 by FOMU Corp.

"It's not that I fail to appreciate lad'ss sspirit," he explained, "but droonge content of vibrationss iss altogether too high for endurance."

"I seem to have a slight case of droonge allergy myself," Retief confided. The two moved back, seated themselves on a flat rock overlooking the enemy approaches, as the rest of the detachment gathered around Len, strumming away as enthusiastically as if he were at a hangar dance back on Blue Moon.

Harrumph heaved a sigh, a sound not unlike the death rattle of a rhino. "Ssuch pity; yoursself, and Ssean and all hiss Terriess—and I as well—musst die, all for vainglory of one madman. If I could but get my handss on hiss sscrawny neck . . ." He clacked his chelae together with a sharp report.

"That might be fun," Retief said. "But how would it help our present situation?"

"Well, it . . ." Harrumph began, then broke off, looked thoughtfully at Retief, his saucer eyes gleaming in the dark. "As matter of fact," he said, "it could change entire complexion of ssituation. Hikop alone iss ressponsible for thiss idiocy. If he were removed . . . !"

"You think his men might break off the attack?"

"It dependss on who steppss in as hiss ssuccessor—but I have a sshrewd notion that only Hikop'ss zeal has been ressponsible for their perssistence in the face of heavy cassualties!"

"Suppose someone picks him off as they charge?"

"No! Hikop iss mine alone to deal with! And anyway, honor would require that charge, once begun, musst be pressed home. But if I could eliminate him *now*, before attack . . ."

"Can you spot him down there?"

"No. I sscanned possition carefully, gun in hand. He iss well concealed. Look for yourself, nothing sstirss below—until the moment of assault!" Harrumph clashed his shredders in frustration. "If it were not sso utterly hopeless, I would try to sneak up on him as he liess in wait—but it would be ssuicide. Better to remain here, and lend my weight to final ressisstance."

"What you need is a diversion," Retief said.

Harrumph made a sardonic sound. "What could possibly divert Hikop'ss hordes from total concentration on bare expanse of rock I would have to cross?" he inquired rhetorically.

"I'm not sure," Retief said. "But I just may have an idea."

"What'ss that? Now, wait, Retief, you can't—"

"Maybe not," the Terran said. "But I'll give it a try." He rose. "Keep it quiet," he said. "Better for morale if nobody knows what I'm up to."

"But—" Harrumph began.

"Just one question," Retief cut in briskly. "What's the simplest way to take a Haterakan out of action without killing him?"

"A sharp blow just here..." Harrumph indicated the juncture where his four arms sprang from his horny chest. "But—"

"Thanks," Retief said and turned and slipped away into the blackness between towering boulders.

12

Retief made his way carefully across the tumbled rock of the Terran position, pausing every few yards to scan the terrain ahead and below. Emerging from a cleft just below the crest of the mound, he wormed his way forward on a dusty ledge, looked down on the broken ground among the declivities in which the Haterakans were concealed, waiting for M minute and S second, to launch their final assault.

A tiny flicker of motion caught Retief's eye, halfway between the enemy line and the base of the mound. He fine-tuned his optical filters for maximum visibility, watched the spot intently. Thirty seconds passed. His eyes began to burn from the incidental radiation pouring into them, along with the small added increment of visible light. There was another flirt of movement; a stealthy, dark shape crept from deep shadow, advanced a dozen feet, disappeared behind a rock slab the size of a grand piano. In the brief glimpse he had had, Retief identified the dark armor of a Haterakan commando.

Directly below Retief's ledge, a shallow trench, probably cut by eons of flowing dust, led downward in an irregular line. He edged forward, slid into the scant concealment, working his way downslope. He had covered ten yards when the infiltrator below appeared again, gained another few feet. Retief left the trough, crossed an exposed ridge, clambered down a rough stairway of broken stones. This time, when he eased forward for a look, the enemy scout was in plain view to him—though apparently invisible to the embattled Terrans above—and not more than twenty feet away.

Retief faded back and waited. Half a minute later, a pebble clattered down from the ridge before him. He inched forward, pulled himself up in time to see the prowler slide behind the shelter of a projecting buttress just above him. With infinite care, Retief backed, ascended ten feet, traversed to a point above the alien's position, and lay flat.

Through the rock he head a faint scrabbling sound. A Haterakan head rose up before him, six feet away. The narrow shoulders followed, and the arms, reaching toward Retief's shadowy hiding place for a grip—

Retief lunged, slammed a fist square into the pressure point described by Harrumph, caught the Haterakan's arms as he folded, dragged him up and into the shelter of the buttress.

The unconscious alien was stripped for action to the bare essentials: vacuum helmet, rank and unit insignia in drab paint, a gun belt with a gun, curiously shaped to fit the alien's boneless fingers, and a single pouch. Retief pried open the latter, came up with a spare power cylinder for the weapon, a fingering stone, a packet of iron rations—and a small tube with a flip-cap.

He opened the latter, tilted it. A small plastic ampule dropped out in his hand. It was identical with the one he had taken from the gas gun wielded by Rukktooey in the cell under the arena of the Haterakan city.

2

Retief thrust the capsule into the atmosphere-test unit mounted under his chin, sniffed cautiously, caught a faint but unmistakable whiff of fresh-crushed mint. Beside him, the downed alien stirred. Swiftly, Retief trussed him in his own harness, then climbed down via a convenient cleft to level ground. As he turned to pick his route, he saw a tall figure stand suddenly, fifty feet away, wave an anterior arm. At once, ungainly Haterakan forms rose up all across the landscape: tens, hundreds of them, with guns at the ready for the advance in an irresistible wave which would sweep across the prominence where the handful of Terrans waited to make their final stand. Even as Retief moved to flatten himself against the nearest rock, a Haterakan loomed behind it. The alien's great eyes goggled through the clear plastic of his helmet. With a convulsive start, he aimed a blow at Retief's head with a lower arm, fumbling at the safety release of his gun. Retief ducked aside, and with a twist of a valve, flooded his helmet with *inth.*

The alien brought his gun around, raised it . . . and froze into immobility. At the same moment, the sky paled as though the house lights had been turned up, bathing the scene in a cold, multicolor glare. Great banners of ashy flame glowed to prominence as Retief's drug-affected optic nerves responded to the unfiltered high-frequency radiation of the star-clotted sky.

Moving with care, he stepped around his would-be assailant, leaned forward, pushed off with a gentle thrust, and floated swiftly over the rocky ground among the statue-like Haterakan troops. He passed within ten feet of the gaudily caparisoned Grand Admiral, standing with his staff in a protected hollow at the rear of the assault line, staring fixedly toward the Terran position. He grounded on a rise, changed direction slightly, and pushed off again. In great fifty- and hundred-foot leaps, Retief left the scene of the impending battle, heading for a spot out of sight beyond a ragged line of peaks.

3

The crater where the recaptured Haterakan ship had exploded lay stark and deserted under the neon sky. Great fragments of the wreck were strewn all about, apparently cold and dark, but actually, to judge from the petrified clouds of gases hanging over them, burning fiercely. There were bodies here, too— Haterakans caught in the blast or gunned down by Sean's Legionnaires—unfortunate sacrifices to their admiral's ambitions.

Retief crossed the crater, found the narrow ravine through

which he had first approached it, emerged in the hollow where the wrecked courier boat had lain, Nothing remained of the little vessel now but crumpled fragments of hull and a chaotic scattering of its contents, the results of enemy gunfire.

Quickly, Retief scanned the ground, turned over chunks of insulation, tangles of wiring, snarls of conduit, half of an acceleration couch, a stack of packaged chicken dinners, hardly damaged, what was left of the auxiliary power unit—and a scorched mailbag, the castastrophe-proof polyon still intact, the seal in place. He hoisted the sack to his shoulder—it weighed no more than an ounce, but the inertia was massive—and headed back for the battlefield at full speed.

Ten subjective minutes had elapsed, Retief estimated, by the time he braked to a halt in the center of the immobile Haterakan assault force. He dumped the bag, broke open the seal, drew out the first of the thick catalogs, and set to work.

4

The *inth,* prevented from dissipating by the enclosing helmet, should produce at least double its previous effective duration, Retief surmised as he completed the first phase of his behind-the-lines attack—which should, he hoped, give him time to complete phase two. He stepped to the nearest Haterakan, flipped up the toggle switch at the side of his helmet. He repeated the action with the next, went on to the next, and the next....

He had dealt with 341 of the enemy soldiers, working in a widening path leading from Admiral Hikop's post at the rear through the ranks to the front, when the first indication of the waning of the *inth* effect became apparent. Retief scanned the sky; the pale wings of light had begun to darken almost imperceptibly toward normal blackness. A Haterakan before him stirred to sluggish motion, bringing a bony leg forward in the first step of the attack. All across the field, the frozen statues began to quicken into life.

Retief aimed himself toward the Terran-held mound, kicked off, shot through the ranks of reviving soldiery. At the base of the mound he leaped upward, aided by the low gravity of the tiny worldlet; a moment later he had regained the ledge from which he had started. Harrumph, just returning to normal motion, was in the act of rising up in alarm at the sight of the charging enemy below. Retief caught the alien's arm as he reached for his helmet switch.

"Whatever you do, don't switch to command channel!" Retief said quickly. "And don't stop to look at anything!"

He hurried forward to where the remnant of the Legion still clustered around Len, not yet aware of the advance. He stepped in, put his helmet against that of the guitar player.

"Len—play that Texas number of yours—and whatever happens, don't stop!"

"Bully, what's—" Sean had leaped up, spun, was staring down at the charging Haterakans. "Get ready, boys! Pick your targets and make every shot count!" As he spoke, the orderly line below wavered, paused, halted—and dissolved into a scene of chaos.

5

"What's got into 'em, Sean?" Harry, too dumfounded to shoot, gaped at the leaping, dancing, wildly gesticulating Haterakans as they threw aside their guns, the charge forgotten, dashed to and fro, colliding with each other, falling to the ground where they lay tearing at their helmets, threshing in compulsive resonance with the blare of Len's earset-amplified guitar.

"Beats me!" Sean yelled. "But now's our chance! Let 'em have it!"

"Hold your fire!" Retief caught Sean's arm, pointed. The tall, fantastic shape of Harrumph was dimly visible halfway down the mound, making for the enemy lines at a full gallop.

"Hey! That's our tame Lobster!" the redhead barked. "Running out on us, is he?" He raised his crater rifle.

Retief knocked it aside and the shot splattered molten rock twenty feet above Harrumph's head. Unheeding, the Haterakan exile scrambled down the last few yards, plunged for the thick of the dithering mob, over which what appeared to be sheets of paper fluttered like oversized confetti.

"What's the idea, Bully? That's a deserter—"

"Hey, Sean!" Lou shouted. "They're retreating!"

Harry jumped up. "Yippee! Let's go after them Lobsters—!"

"Stand fast!" Sean roared, staring down in astonishment at

the spectacle of the entire enemy corps precipitatedly fleeing the scene at top speed—those who were not kicking their rhythmic last, their helmets ripped from their heads in their struggles. In half a minute the last of the surviving Haterakans had dragged himself from the stricken field.

"You can stop playing, now, Len," Retief called to the boy, still intent on his strumming. "We've beaten off the first wave, at least."

6

"The next move is up to them," Sean said grimly. "We'll sit tight and see what happens."

"They won't be back," Harry exulted. "Boy, just the idea of coming up against the Legion was too much for 'em, the yellowbellies!"

"If we don't get some rations and water from someplace pretty quick, we're done for anyway," Lou muttered.

"Yeah—that is kind of a problem area, ain't it, Sean?" Len spoke up. "And I need a new E string for my guitar, too."

"Hey—lookit there!" Jack Raskall pointed. From the rocky ridge over which the Haterakans had launched their aborted assault, a lone alien wearing a crested headdress staggered into view, making his way toward the Terran position. Over his head, a scrap of white cloth dangled from a bent metal rod.

"Don't shoot," Sean ordered. "Looks like a big shot—under a flag of truce!"

"Wonder what he wants?" Clem queried.

"That's easy!" Len said excitedly. "They're surrendering! Giving up! We won!"

"Not so fast, Len," Sean cautioned. "There's still a hundred of them for every one of us!"

The Haterakan reached the base of the mound, started up. The Terrans watched in silence as he scaled the tumbled rocks, drew himself up over the final edge and rose, dusting himself off, a bedraggled figure marked with the bruises and scars of recent combat.

"Hey," Len said. "Ain't that—?"

"Shh!" Sean motioned him to silence as the alien lowered a sack fashioned from a torn garment to the ground, opened it, shook it. An object rolled out; it was the size of a ripe pumpkin, sheathed in horn, adorned with broken spines. It stopped with its great lifeless eyes staring blankly up at the endless sky.

"Behold mortal remainss of Hikop, once Grand Admiral," Harrumph's unmistakable voice croaked. "Sslain by mysself in ssingle combat!"

7

"I caught him there, where the tall stones lean together." Harrumph waved an upper arm. "He fought valiantly for hiss life, as befitss noble of Haterakan race. But *I* fought for more than life! I gave battle in name of honor!"

"Looks like he put up quite a scrap," Jack Raskall noted as the battered victor tottered to a seat on a flat rock.

"Disspossing of Hikop was mere trifle," Harrumph replied. "But on the way back I inadvertently caught glimpse of page out of catalog, with full-color illo of Cr.69.98 living-room suite. Ugh! Thosse obsscene upholsstery patternss were nearly death of me! Between those, and Len's droonge tones, attackers were helpless!" He goggled a bloodshot eye at Retief. "Little did Hikop ssusspect, when he put you to torment, Bully, that one day you'd return his own techniques against him!"

"Then—with old Hikop dead—I guess the war's over!" Jack spoke in tones of wonderment. "Just like that! All we got to do now is get off this hunk o' rock and tuck into some vittles—"

"Just a minute," Sean cut in. He turned to the alien. "You did O.K., Rumpy. Now, suppose you go back down and talk to whoever's taken over from Hikop, see about calling a truce, and giving us a boat, and—"

"Ah, perhapss you fail to undersstand, Ssean," Harrumph raised a claw. "I am slayer of Grand Admiral. I am also highest ranking Haterakan in naval forces, now that he hass ssuffered ssad demise. Ergo—*I* am ssuccessor and New Grand Admiral!"

Sean looked perplexed for a moment, then brightened. "Well, hell, that settles that! You just give me your formal surrender, and we can all quit and go home!"

"It iss not quite sso ssimple as that, General Braze!" the Haterakan said sternly. "As Grand Admiral, I have ssole ressponsibility for Haterakan forcess! And peace-lover though I am, honor forbidss that Haterakan fighting force ssubmit to capture by mere handful of Terranss! No!" he clacked his shredders decisively. "It iss I who musst demand ssurrender of yoursself and all your men!"

"Huh?" Sean frowned darkly while his hands tightened on the grips of his rifle. "You've got the gall to walk in here—you, supposed to be a friend of ours—and call on me to give up?"

"Alass, I expect you to fight to death," Harrumph cut in. "But I musst give you chance, out of regard for our former association."

"Lobster, you better get back down that slope and under cover as fast as your trotters will carry you," Sean grated. "And take that truce flag with you!"

"I regret you fail to appreciate change in circumstancess," Harrumph said sadly. "However—I sshall personally ssee to it your remainss are shipped home for grinding into fertilizer—or whatever you Terriess do with leftovers. It iss leasst I can do for gallant defenderss of hopeless possition."

"Git, damn you!" Sean snapped.

"Mind your tone," Harrumph came back sharply. "After all, as one of thosse ssame defenders, I desserve a little consideration! Actually, it'ss something of *coup* on my part," he added as he turned to lower himself over the ledge, "to have played role both in heroic last-ditch defense and glorious victory of my sside—my *new* sside."

"Before you hurry away, Grand Admiral," Retief said, "I'd like a word with you. I think you're overlooking a point or two."

"I know what you are thinking, my dear former comrade," the alien sighed. "I'm well aware that cheap victory now will be paid for in end by crusshing defeat at handss of vasst Terran fleetss, aroussed by massacre of Legion. But that's way cookie crumbless. After brave ssacrificess of my troops, I could hardly deprive them of their moment of glory!"

"In my experience most combat soldiers are more interested in loot than glory," Retief countered smoothly.

"True..." Harrumph glanced at the handful of haggard Terrans in their grimy mismatched garments. "But I fear there iss little to be had here in way of sspoilss of war."

"However," Retief went on, "if you play your cards right, I think there might just be a possibility, in spite of this little misunderstanding, of rectifying that situation."

Harrumph cocked his head. "You are prepared to pay ranssomss, perhaps?"

"Not precisely," Retief said. He turned to Sean. "With your permission, General, I'd like to take the Admiral aside for a moment."

"Go ahead," Sean grunted. "I guess we've got nothing to lose—so long as you remember our motto: the Legion dies, but never surrenders."

"Quite so," Retief inclined his head. "Now, Admiral," he said to Harrumph, "let me tell you about your PAUPER program...."

8

Thirty-six hours later, in the rustic, antler-decorated Grand Hall of the Headquarters of the Terran Defense Legion at Blue Moon, Grand Admiral Harrumph signed the Articles of Capitulation on behalf of the combined Haterakan Fleets.

"It iss asstonisshing," he said as he penned his name and titles with a series of flourishes, "that fruits of defeat turn out to be ssweeter than victory."

"Just sign these other nineteen copies, and the foundations of a fruitful Haterakan-Terran future will have been laid," First Secretary Bloodblister cooed, offering a sheaf of red-sealed and -taped documents.

"That'ss all very well," Harrumph paused, pen upraised, to stare suspiciously at the diplomat. "But when does firsst sshipment of goodiess arrive?"

"Just as soon as you Haterakans have withdrawn your fleets to the agreed-on positions." Bloodblister wagged a playful finger. "We don't want you to be tempted to sweep up any little crumbs that might seem to be lying around loose."

"Hah!" Sean grunted from his position far down the table, where he had been shunted by the swarm of CDT functionaries who had arrived to supervise the armistice. "Those crumbs that cookie-cutter's talking about are the frontier worlds!" He turned to Retief who, still wearing his frontier garb and three-day stubble, had passed unrecognized by his compatriots of the Corps Diplomatique. "We do all the fighting, and these Johnnies step in and take over like they owned the Universe—"

"We invited them," Retief reminded the big redhead mildly. "You might say we were lucky that cruising Peace Enforcer saw fit to regard us as victorious patriots instead of pirates."

Sean's fist hit the table hard enough to make the ashtrays jump.

"Lucky!" he boomed, then lowered his tone as half a dozen icy diplomatic glares turned his way.

"Now, Grand Admiral," a small, shoulderless Second Secretary in a faultlessly cut midafternoon puce seersucker dickey and ocher velvet tailcoat said unctuously in the silence, "if you'll just let us know if there's anything else you want...?"

Sean snorted, rose and stamped across to the fireplace, where he stood, feet braced apart, hands behind his back, muttering to himself until the scratching of pens and the fluttering of mutual assurances of esteem had ended and the diplomats had buckled up their briefcases and departed for their waiting vessel, accompanied by Harrumph and his aides.

"I'm glad to see the last of that crowd of meat-eating canaries!" the big man barked as the door closed on the harassed Third Secretary bringing up the rear. "By the devil's adenoids, if we'd left it up to that bunch, we'd all be pulling an oar in a Haterakan river barge; and now that we've beaten the Lobsters back with our blood, sweat, and lighter fluid, they chum up to 'em like long-lost creditors—and leave without even saying toodle-oo!"

"It wasn't exactly a victory of arms," Retief reminded the irate general. "The spirit of the Legion left nothing to be desired—but if Harrumph hadn't seen the wisdom of a truce, the next charge would have ironed us out like a lace hanky."

"Maybe," Sean said flatly. "But things are a little different, now. The CDT blockade's lifted; those troops from Jawbone and the other worlds can join up. We can get all the men we want! All I've go to do is yell, and they'll come pouring in from all across the frontier with ships and armaments—everything we need!"

"Need for what, Sean?" Retief inquired. "The war's over."

"Is it?" Sean shot him a sharp look, turned to stare into the fire. "Who says so, the CDT? What's the CDT to me? A bunch of pencil-pushers who left us to sink or swim when the pressure was on, and jumped in to grab the glory as soon as we'd turned the tide." He whirled, his face set in lines of hard determination.

"Those triple-damned diplomats left the Lobsters with their fleets intact! And you saw the truce lines they drew! Just a hop and a skip from every Terry world on the frontier! As soon as the Lobsters have collected all the pretties they want—blooie! They'll hit the whole line at once like a ton of anvils, boot us off our worlds and then thumb their olfactory tendrils at the CDT— until they come running, with a new load of concessions!"

"I don't think so, Sean," Retief said. "Now that the CDT has signatures on a formal agreement, it can't afford to let the Haterakans stir up any trouble. If they did, half the would-be land-grabbers in this end of the Western Arm would start trying their wings. Beside which, I think we can trust Harrumph—"

"I don't trust any alien any farther than I can lever him with a crowbar!" Sean came back hotly. "Whose side are you on, anyway, West? I seem to remember seeing you disappear just before the Lobsters chickened out on their last charge. It wouldn't be that you're working both sides of the street, would it?"

"Hey, Sean," Harry spoke up. "That ain't no way to talk to Bully—"

"I'll talk any way I like!" Sean bellowed. "And that's enough of this first-name stuff! It's General Braze from now on!" He yanked his formerly splended tunic into line with a jangle of battle-stained medals, a tall, martial figure with fire in his eye.

"It's time to look at the situation realistically." He swept his assembled veterans with a fierce look. "We all know the Lobsters haven't been beaten—just stopped, for the moment. As soon as they get on the prod again, it'll be Waterhole all over again!" He smacked a huge fist into a horny palm. "We've been sold down the river by the CDT! To them, we're just chips in a card game—and it's a game we can't win! So, by the devil's ulcers, we'll play it our way! Let's face it: with the whole frontier behind us, we're the strongest force in this end of the Galaxy— unless we let those redtape artists disarm us! Are we going to sit still for that?"

"Hell, no!" someone yelped.

"Not us, General!" other voices chimed in.

"Yeah, but—" a lone dissenter began, but was drowned in the general enthusiasm.

"The time to act is now!" Sean's voice rang like massed trumpets. "The Legion is armed and ready! We've had a taste of

Lobster justice—and CDT betrayal! But we don't have to stand for it! We've got the men and the ships and the guns: have we got the guts?"

"You bet, Sean!"

"Count on us!"

Sean raised his hands for silence as the clamor rose, the men gathering around, eager looks replacing the glum letdown of the moment before.

"All right, boys," he shouted. "Let the CDT print up all the fancy papers it wants to: by the time those bureaucrats know what's happened, we'll have run the Lobsters right out of the cluster! Hell, right out of the Arm!" He paused for a wild cheer. "And after that—hell, why stop there? There's plenty of other worlds out there that we Terries could use—and the E.T.'s are squatting on too damn many of 'em! We can change all that! After we've cleaned out the cluster, we'll hit Gumpert IV next; there's a bunch of nine-legged jack rabbits out there cluttering up the place!" His eyes glowed with the prospects. "There's no telling where it could end!"

"Sure there is," Retief said loudly. The cheering died as the men turned to him expectantly. He drew on his dope-stick and blew out a casual plume of smoke.

"It ends right here," he said flatly.

"What's that?" Sean rapped in the shocked silence.

"It's all a pipe dream, Sean," Retief said. "I think the men have had enough military glory to last them. The Legion has served its purpose. It's time to disband it and let everybody get back to what he was doing before all this got started."

"Disband? Go home?" Sean tornadoed. "Are you out of your mind? I'm holding the cluster in my hand like a ripe apple! You expect me to toss it away?"

Retief stood, faced the big redhead, eye to eye.

"What it boils down to, Sean," he said, "is that you've got a bad case of ambition, complicated by visions of empire."

Sean stared at him triumphantly. "I'm the strongest man in the cluster!" he boomed. "It's not only my right—it's my duty to use that strength!" He half-turned to shout an order to Lou, standing by eagerly.

"Wrong again, Sean," Retief said; the war chief turned as though stung by a wasp.

"What's that supposed to mean, West?" he barked.

"You're not the toughest man in the cluster, Sean," Retief said. He tossed his dope-stick into the fire and looked the other in the eye. "You're not even the toughest man in this room. . . ."

A profound silence fell as all eyes held on the two big men.

Sean nodded suddenly. "I get it at last," he grated. "You've got an idea you can take over, is that it, West? Well, I guess now is as good a time as any to settle that!"

"I guess it is, Sean," Retief said.

"Clear the floor!" Sean roared, the light of battle in his eyes. With a sudden surge, he ripped off the battle-scarred tunic and tossed it aside with a clash of medals, exposing brawny arms, a massive red fuzzed chest ribbed with muscles like oak roots. "All right, West! Just you and me, fair and square! Nobody interferes, nobody yells for help—no matter what!" He glared around at the watching ring of men. "Because only one of us is going to walk out of here alive!"

13

"Wait a minute, Sean," Len spoke up. "This is no time for us to start scrapping amongst ourselves—"

"Let's do this right!" Lou's voice blanketed the youngster's. "General, as challenged party, you've got the choice of weapons—"

Sean raised a pair of fists like bare-knuckled picnic hams. "These are all the weapons I'll need! Out of the way, Lou—" He brushed the big-nosed man aside, stepped forward and threw a straight left past Retief's head, crossed it with a whistling right hook which just missed, leaned aside as Retief feinted with a right to the head—and *oof!*ed as the punch changed direction, smacked home against his ribs. A shout went up—rose higher as Sean backed a step, threw a roundhouse left and right, both missing as Retief ducked; then the redhead bored in, slamming an uppercut that failed to connect, took a straight right on the forearm, drove a right in past Retief's guard to catch him on the chest—and rocked back as Retief landed a solid right to the jaw.

"Paste him, Sean!" someone yelled as the big redhead backpedaled, shaking his head, then rallied, fended off a pair of left jabs and charged. Retief slammed a left and right against the rebel general's chest, but the latter's lunge carried him in to cannon against Retief; he wrapped his arms around the other, bore him backward into the table. The heavy board screeched, sliding back across rough stonework; then a leg gave way, and the pair went down across it in a clatter of ale pots and splintering lumber—and broke apart as Retief's elbow came up under Sean's chin with an audible *whok!*

Back on their feet, they circled—two slim-waisted, broad-shouldered heavyweights, Sean overtopping Retief's six three by an inch and a half. Aside from a red blotch on the side of Sean's jaw, neither was marked.

"You're good at dodging, Bully, I'll give you that," Sean grunted. "But that won't—" He broke off as Retief stepped in, laced a right hook across his jaw, and was out again before the redhead had completed his counterpunch. Sean shook his head, grinned harshly.

"That the best you can do, Bully? Hell, I—" With a speed surprising in a two-hundred-and-forty pounder, Sean punctuated his own comment with a pounce and a straight right that ricocheted off Retief's guard to slam home against his shoulder, followed with a left hook that sizzled past Retief's chin as he leaned back, countering with a left hook of his own that caught Sean on the ear, sent him reeling past. As Retief spun to follow, Sean whirled, drove a left in under Retief's right elbow and, as the latter pivoted away, followed with a second left to the shoulder, a right that met an upraised arm, another left that glanced off Retief's left fist—

With a solid *whok-whok!* Retief pounded a right and a left to Sean's head that drove the bigger man back to slam through a half-open hall door. Retief followed up, landed another hearty right, took a pair of jabs to the short ribs, then shot a straight left in under the redhead's guard to jolt against his jaw. Sean staggered, backed, covering up, countering with left jabs. Still backing, he collided with a closed door, which flew wide as the lock splintered from the frame, and they were in the kitchen, circling a wide table where a haunch of venison lay, a heavy cleaver beside it. Retief saw Sean's eyes flick to the weapon; but the general bypassed it, to seize the table and shove it hard at Retief. As the latter jumped back, Sean leaped the barrier, barreled full-tilt into him, carrying both of them crashing into the crowd just surging in through the broken door.

Clear again, with Harry nursing a bruised ear in the background, Retief moved in, took a light tap on the head, slammed a right to Sean's stomach. As the big man grunted and covered up, he hit him twice on the head, glancingly; Sean backed, caromed off the wall, and rebounded, swinging lefts and rights. One connected, sent Retief back against a Dutch door. The upper half banged opened, and a gust of icy air whirled in, bearing a swirl of snow. Sean charged, head down—and Retief slid aside. The redhead checked, too late, smashed through the door into the yard. Retief jumped after him, caught him on the side of the head with a right hook that sent Sean to his knees in a drift of snow as the ringsiders poured outside, howling and yippeeing.

Sean shook his head, came to his feet in a rush, grappled with Retief, tying up his arms. Retief leaned hard, freed his right, sank a solid punch to Seans' ribs. Then they were apart, circling again, as the watching men shouted encouragement to both parties impartially.

"Missed an opening then, didn't you, Bully?" Sean grunted.

"You've taught me to be suspicious of easy targets, Sean," Retief replied. "That stumbling act was nearly a winner."

"It never failed before." Sean smiled, showing white teeth. He moved in, his guard up, more cautious now, but still the aggressor, still as strong as ever in spite of a slight increase in his breathing rate. Retief watched him, met an upraised arm the size of a rolled carpet—and threw a straight right that whistled in past Sean's left, connected with the redhead's jaw—

A blinding flash of lightning, and a dull *boom!* of thunder, and the deck was tilting underfoot, rotating like a merry-go-round. Retief planted his feet, leaned against the sway of the planking, blinked through the misty fog that filled the air. The rumble of thunder rolled, sharpened, transmuted into the roar of yelling men. Six feet away, Sean stood swaying, his arms hanging loose at his sides. Retief took a step, raised his hands, took aim—and missed as Sean wobbled aside. Retief turned, his head still ringing like the carillon at Notre Dame, located his opponent, watched a wild haymaker sail past two feet away, stepped in and planted a left-right against the other's ribs.

The impact seemed to arouse Sean. He backed unsteadily,

shook himself, halted, went into a defensive stance against which Retief's left-right-left pounded fruitlessly.

"Pretty good sock...you landed..." Sean was breathing hard now. "But not quite...good enough."

"I think we broke even on that one." Retief jabbed, ducked under a right hook, missed with a right, took a left on the biceps, got through with a left jab, stepped back. The redhead followed, blood dripping from his chin, his chest, shiny with perspiration, rising and falling with his panting breath.

"Blast you, Bully, stand and fight!" Sean panted.

"Yeah, let's see some action!" a man yelled from the sidelines.

With a curse, Sean closed, swung a wild right. Retief jumped aside, stepped in behind it, and right-hooked the redhead on the side of the jaw. Sean went to his knees. The audience went wild. Looking up, the redhead blinked, then tottered to his feet.

"Just wait until I land one good punch, Bully," he said blurrily. "Just one good punch!"

"Come and deliver it," Retief said. "I'll be right here."

Sean nodded. "You've got guts, Bully. Too bad you got too big for your breeches." With a grim smile he moved in. His left shot out—and Retief's crossed it; both blows landed at once—and were followed by a second, a third. Standing toe to toe, the two men slammed trip-hammer blows, left, right, left, to chest, midriff, jaw. Blood started from Sean's cut mouth, was splattered away as his head rocked to Retief's pounding and all the while, Sean's big, businesslike fists worked, driving against Retief's body, *whap, whap, whap....*

And then the big redhead shifted his right foot, staggered; for a moment he caught himself; then a devastating right hook to the jaw jerked his head half around to meet a left that snapped it back; and then he was leaning, his fists driving against nothing, sliding past Retief's shoulder, going down like a felled oak with a slam that seemed to shake the frozen ground.

A long sigh went up from the watching men. Standing over his opponent, Retief swayed, shook his head, then with an effort, stood erect.

"Well, gentlemen," he said blurrily, "I think the general has decided to see it my way."

2

"Don't take it too hard, Sean," Retief said an hour later as he stood with the former general in the cavernous entry of the old farmhouse. "In time I think you'll see the wisdom of letting sleeping Lobsters lie."

"Maybe," the big man grunted through puffed lips. There were half a dozen patches of tape on his face, his nose was swollen, and one eye was a puffy black and blue. "But to hell with that: you beat me fair and square. No hard feelings?" He thrust out a big square fist, which Retief gripped heartily.

"It's going to be kind of a letdown, going back to farming, after all this." Sean waved a hand in a vague gesture which somehow took in battle fleets, gold braid, medals, and comradeship around a roaring fire. "Still, maybe the boys and I can get together now and again to talk over old times." His tone brightened a shade. "We held 'em at Waterhole, anyway, didn't we, Bully? They can't take that away from us."

"That's right, Sean—and something tells me that your talents aren't going to be allowed to go to waste."

Sean eyed Retief quizzically. "You know, Bully, somehow I've got a feeling that there's more to you than you let on. But I'm not prying. I guess a man's past is his own business."

"The past is just a collection of false impressions," Retief said. "It's the future that I'm looking forward to." Ten minutes later, Retief lifted off in the thirty-foot space skiff with which Sean had presented him as a parting gift; clear of the atmosphere, he scanned nearby space, picked up a lone blip representing a small ship hovering in a ten-thousand-mile orbit. "Right on the job," Retief murmured, and set his course so as to pass within fifty miles of the stranger, then switched on his comm screen, set it at CDT frequency.

Ten minutes passed before a voice crackled suddenly from the panel: "You there in the skiff! Heave to! You won't be warned twice!"

He flipped on the vision channel; the grim face of an Emporium Planetary Police officer stared out at him—and over the other's shoulder, the pinched features of First Secretary Bloodblister goggled.

"Yes—I'm sure," the diplomat said breathlessly. "That's him—"

"O.K.," the cop barked. "Don't try anything smart, you! You're under arrest for murder!"

3

Three pairs of cold eyes bored into Retief, standing before his inquisitors with a pair of heavy cuffs clamping his wrists.

"... and, in addition to the crimes for which you have already been condemned to death, in absentia," Consul General Foulbrood was saying, "is now added the further heinous charge of murder!"

"By the way, who did I murder?" Retief inquired conversationally, at which the armed guard at his back prodded him with a short-barreled power gun.

The Consul glanced sideways at Bloodblister, past him at the suety features of Assistant Interior Minister Overdog, back at Retief.

"In the course of your illegal departure from confinement, you viciously slaughtered at least nine guards in cold blood," he stated in a flat tone.

"Retief!" Bloodblister gasped. "How could you!"

"That's what I was wondering," Retief said, eliciting another sharp jab in the back. He turned.

"Touch me again with that, Sonny," he said easily to the slack-jawed warder, "and I'll bend it around your neck."

"You see?" Foulbrood blurted as the startled jailer started back. "The man's a mad dog! Enemies are all about us, gentlemen! And so long as the criminal lives, all our lives are in danger!"

"Lives in danger?" Bloodblister's eyebrows went up. "I hardly see—"

"But *I* see through his schemes!" Foulbrood touched a pale tongue to thin lips. "For that reason, by authority of the powers vested in me, I order that the prisoner be taken to the armory and there summarily dealt with in accordance with—"

"Just a minute!" Bloodblister gasped as the guard motioned Retief toward a side door. "You mean—shoot him? Just like that?"

"Of course," Overdog spoke up, rubbing his hands together briskly. "No sense in dawdling, eh, Foulbrood? So if—"

"But...but...I protest! The man, for all his deficiencies, is an official of the Corps Diplomatique! True, he was condemned by a provincial Planetary court, but in deep space such a finding can hardly be considered as legal. If I'd had any idea you planned anything of this sort, I'd never have consented to act as...as..."

"Fingerman, I believe the term is, Mr. Bloodblister," Retief supplied, as the guard snarled and gestured menacingly.

"I think on reflection you'll find we're on firm ground," Foulbrood snapped. "If there are no further objections, I think we can adjourn now and be in time for first lunch call—"

There was a clatter in the corridor, a shrill voice raised in indignant command. A moment later the outer door flew wide and the slight figure of Undersecretary Magnan burst into the room, yanking his lapels in line. His sharp gaze swept the room, ignored Retief, half through the side door, impaled Foulbrood as the latter opened his mouth.

"You, sir! Are you responsible for this outrage?"

"You—you mean, the, ah, hearing...?" Foulbrood stuttered, clutching at the papers before him.

"The specific outrage to which I was referring was the total lack of protocol accorded me since my arrival aboard this vessel half an hour ago! Why, I had to seek you out unassisted! Not only unassisted, but actually impeded by armed persons!" He glared at the guard standing in the doorway looking dumfounded.

"Hey, chief," the man started. "This jasper—"

Recovering himself, Foulbrood gestured the fellow to silence. "Just who are you, sir?" he demanded. "I happen to be conducting an official inquiry into matters of grave import, and—"

"Tish-tush, my man!" Magnan said sternly. "If you'd read my TWX, you'd have been aware of my impending visit!"

"This—this is Undersecretary Magnan, from Sector," Bloodblister choked, mopping his forehead. "Goodness, Mr. Magnan, what are you doing w-way out here?"

"Reports have reached my ears of certain events on a minor world known as Emporium," the senior diplomat replied chillingly. "You, sir"—he glanced at Overdog—"are a functionary in the local government there, I believe?" He swung to face Foulbrood. "While *you* are Principal Officer of the CDT Mission there, correct?"

"Why, ah, as to that—"

"Spare me your protestations." Magnan dropped his briefcase on the table, pulled out a chair, seated himself, placed his fingertips together, and gazed coldly at the two men.

"Now, gentlemen—suppose you start at the beginning and tell me all of the circumstances surrounding the rather bizarre events of the last few days!"

4

". . . and that's all there is to it, Mr. Undersecretary." Foulbrood offered a crafty curve of bloodless lips in lieu of a smile. "Under the circumstances and in view of the critical situation interplanetary-tensionwise, I deemed it politic not to interfere with the disposition of the agent provocateur in accordance with local custom. After all, the man was culpably guilty of espionage, sabotage, persiflage, and—"

"Camouflage," Magnam said crisply.

"Eh? Oh, you mean his use of an alias." Fouldbrood nodded complacently. "Yes, I—"

"I mean the entire affair, sir!" Magnan drummed his fingers on his briefcase, gave Foulbrood an ominous look. "Just what is it you're covering up, Mr. Foulbrood? And you, Mr. Overdog!" He shot a look at the plump minister. "Just what were these matters of security into which you accuse Mr. Retief of snooping? And, I might ask, *whose* security? Your own, perhaps?"

"Why, why, why, whatever do you mean, Mr. Undersecretary?" Overdog sputtered, while Foulbrood's expression glazed over like hardening jello.

"It couldn't be, I suppose, gentlemen," Magnan purred, "that you were involved in a scheme to convey military intelligence to the Haterakans, in return for promises of large orders for munitions? Or that certain proposed trade agreements had already been secretly entered into, predicated on the assumption of a Haterakan take-over of the frontier worlds, eh—the while you carried out piratical attacks on Terran interworld shipping,

to be laid at the doorstep of the betrayed frontiersmen..."
Magnun poonched out his lips, stared coldly from one of the
speechless men to the other.

"Enough of this beating about the bush," he said. "Thanks to
a coded dispatch from Mr. Retief, I took the precaution of
visiting Emporium for a few hours, in company with a special
CDT inspection team. I have in my briefcase complete docu-
mentation of the entire unsavory affair—sufficient evidence to
place both of you—and all your accomplices— in durance vile
for the forseeable future—"

"Kransnik—Lutchwell!" Foulbrood snapped his fingers and
the two guards in the room jumped to his side, guns ready. The
consul pointed a shaking finger at Magnan, whose mouth
opened into a lopsided O and froze that way. "Shoot this spy
down!"

Bloodblister yelped and dived for cover. Overdog started up
from his seat. The two guns came around—

From where he was standing, ignored, at the side of the
room, Retief took three quick steps, caught the two armed men
by the backs of their collars and slammed their heads together
with a sound like overripe melons hitting linoleum. As they
slumped, Overdog bleated, made a dash for the door, tripped
over the outflung leg of one of the fallen gunners and went down
hard, to come up with blood streaming through his fingers from
a bruised nose.

"Great heavens, Retief!" Magnan wheezed, flopping back,
limp, in his chair. "For a moment I thought you'd missed your
cue!"

"He did indeed!" Foulbrood snarled, kicking his chair back
and rising, a tiny vest-pocket needler glinting in his bony hand.
"Very clever work, Mr. Undersecretary. A pity it's all wasted.
My crew are loyal—meaning well-paid—and in an hour this
vessel will be across the frontier and into Haterakan territory. I
have friends there—also well-paid. Thanks to our mutual friend,
Mr. Bloodblister, I'm well aware of the disbanding of the so-
called Terran Defense Legion. A new, determined Haterakan
assault now will reverse the position quite neatly—and next time
it will be *my* little group who dictates peace!"

"You're a fool!" Magnan gasped. "I've already filed my
report! Your role in this dastardly affair is already known—"

Foulbrood dismissed the remark with an airy wave of his

hand. "You're as aware as I that the Corps will accept the *fait accompli*. As for my popularity among my fellow Terrestrials—that, Mr. Secretary, is a luxury I've never enjoyed." He raised the gun, took careful aim at Magnan's chest—

"No!" Bloodblister screeched, and lunged from his position, under the table, missed as Foulbrood jumped back quickly. The latter took aim again—

"I'll have to ask you to give me that." Magnan rose and stepped calmly toward Foulbrood. On the other side of the table, Retief saw the renegade consul's finger tighten on the firing stud . . .

The gun went off with a whispery hiss. Magnan checked as the burst of needles plunked at his jacket front; he looked down at a tear in the purple cloth.

"Tsk!" he said, reached and lifted the gun from the astounded plotter's nerveless fingers and laid it gently on the blotter.

"I had a feeling this chest armor might be useful in dealing with a bounder of your stripe." he sniffed. Behind him, the door swung in. A pair of Marines with CDT shoulder tabs stepped into the room.

"All secure, sir." One of them touched his cap to Magnan, swept the room with a quick glance, returned to attention.

"Very good, Albert," the Undersecretary said blandly. "You may take these two along and lock them up." He indicated Foulbrood and Overdog. "As for you, Retief," he added in an aside as the Marines took over, "I think you and I had best sit down together for a few minutes and agree on a story   that is," he corrected himself, "finalize the details of my report."

"Good idea, Mr. Secretary," Retief said. "And while we're at it, I have a couple of proposals for tying up some loose ends."

5

"On the whole, I think the affair turned out rather well," Magnan said in a complacent tone, twirling the stem of his champagne-colored soda-water glass between his fingers, and glancing about contentedly at the glittering crowd thronging the mirrored Grand Reception Hall at Sector HQ. "The frontier is pacified, the settlers have been assured of territorial integrity, the Haterakans are firmly enrolled in the roster of our allies—at least as long as the supply of trade goods lasts— the PAUPER agreement has been signed, I'm in line for my full Undersecretaryship, and you've successfully avoided being court-martialed."

"A diplomatic triumph all along the line," Retief agreed. "Too bad we couldn't include your bulletproof vest in the report. It would have added a whole new dimension to your personnel profile."

"Good heavens, Retief, never mention it!" Magnan glanced critically at Retief's face. "I'm happy to see your bruises are about gone. I trust they're the only remaining evidence of your rather rude variety of diplomacy."

"Except for the other guy," a hearty voice boomed as the tall, wide figure of Sean Braze loomed up beside them, with Lisobel, radiantly gowned, on his arm. Magnan inclined his head to the girl, smiled somewhat sourly at the former general, eyeing the scarlet tunic with its silver aiguillettes, three rows of medals, gold Guards' buttons and Austrian knots, the broad silver-mesh belt buckled with a black and gold eagle, the black jodhpurs with their gold satin stripe, the polished silver-spurred black boots.

"I see you've lost no time in designing ceremonial garments suitable to your new post, Mr. Braze," the Undersecretary said primly. "At Corps expense, I assume?"

"You don't expect the new Grand Exalted Commander of The Veterans of Unfought Wars to go around looking like a hobo, do you, Magnan?" The big redhead lifted a glass from a passing tray. "Here's to all the boys that would have gone to bat for home and hearth if they'd had to!" he toasted.

"Hiya, Bully, fellers." Jack Raskall pushed between two portly matrons and grinned at the group. "I mean, uh, Retief," he amended. "I can't get used to you having two names. Hey, Sean—did you tell him about our new gunboats—"

"Not gunboats, Jack," Sean corrected. "Floats, Remember?" He tossed back his drink, replaced it with a new one offered by a waiter at his elbow. "We're planning lots of parades," he confided as Magnan gasped, nonplused. "We figure to run one past the Hatracks every month or so. And you can't have a parade without floats. We've rigged ours up pretty nifty, with lots of big cardboard guns and torpedoes showing. From a little ways off, you'd swear they were the real thing. As a matter of fact," he added offhandedly, "in a pinch we could make a switch to functioning hardware in a hurry, if we had to. We figure the show'll impress the dickens out of those Lobsters—and it'll give the boys something to do, to keep their minds off all those war reparations they didn't get, thanks to the CDT."

"War reparations!" Magnan sniffed. "Why, you're lucky you haven't been assessed for indemnification of the Haterakans for the loss of half a dozen minor moons to which, candidly, they had at least as good a claim as the Terrestrial settlers—"

"No need, my dear ssir!" a hoarse croak sounded over the heads of the surrounding crowd. The tall, weird figure of a Haterakan elbowed the Groaci counselor aside, brandishing a glass of cherry brandy in one hand and using the other three manipulatory members to keep a tall shako in position on his head. "With sstream of prettiess now flowing in through good offices of PAUPER, there'ss no point in our making pigss of ourselvess, eh?" Harrumph eyed Sean's uniform.

"Hmmm. Not bad—though little on drab side," he assessed. "Perhaps you wouldn't mind lending me name of your tailor, eh, Sean?"

"Sure." Sean scanned the alien's pink head-quills, chromed helmet with green horsehair plume, short ocher jacket, powder blue pants and orange imitation alligator open-toed sandals. "I think he could give you a couple of tips on color combinations."

"No need; ssection of sspectrum to which Haterakan ocularss are ressponssive iss quite invissible to you Terriess, I fear."

"I wondered why you jokers could see in the dark," Sean mused. "You boys sure gave my gunners fits when you were infiltrating our position for that final push."

"Frankly, my dear Sean, our troopss were appalled at accuracy of your ssmall-armss fire."

"I have to give you Lobsters credit," Sean grunted. "You know how to take it and come back for more."

Harrumph wagged his head, causing his plumes and quills to clack and rustle. "I must ssay, we were forced to admit you Terriess are formidable antagonisstss . . ."

The two military men sauntered off, deep in mutual congratulation.

"Well," Lisobel sighed. "I suppose he won't remember me for an hour now! I don't know why I waste time on him! He's just an overgrown schoolboy!"

"Two overgrown schoolboys," Magnan sniffed. "The kind who'll never grow up!"

"If they did, the diplomacy racket would get pretty dull." Retief raised his glass. "Here's hoping they never do."

For a moment, Lisobel pouted; then she smiled and raised her glass. Magnan hesitated, then turned to a passing waiter, exchanged his soda water for a stiff scotch on the rocks. Smiling wryly, he joined in the clicking of glasses.

Together, they drank.